Well Versed 2018

Prose and Poetry

Columbia Chapter of the Missouri Writers' Guild

Managing Editors:

Margaret Maginness and Charles Tutt

Well Versed 2018

Table of Contents

Nonfiction . . . . *Nonfiction Judge, Jocelyn Cullity* 76

Poetry . . . . *Poetry Judge, Walter Bargen* 108

Well Versed Sponsors

We would like to extend are hearty thank you to our volunteers. Without these people, there would be no *Well Versed*.

Amy Christianson
Cortney Daniels
Sharon Feltman
Millie Henry
Frank Montagnino
Deb Sutton
Jana Stephens
Lori Younker
Cami Wheeler

Foreword by the President

This anthology has it all. Science fiction, beautiful short stories, thought provoking poetry, and wayward flamingoes. But wait, there's more! Much more. The authors in this book poured their hearts into their creations and while I appreciate the tears I try to hold back when reading, I also appreciate the laughter I cannot. One theme you'll find woven throughout this book is the constant struggle to belong. This is something writers often know about firsthand since writing can be a lonely business. The Columbia Writer's Guild has become a home to myself and many of the authors in this book. I am proud to be a part of such a diverse and talented group of writers.

I hope you enjoy this anthology. May it inspire you to write your own story.

—Debra K. Sutton

Preface by the Editor

Producing *Well Versed* is no small task and involves the collaboration of many members and the donation of time from our recruited judges. It's not always easy or fun, but it is rewarding. This is my second year working on the anthology, and I am proud to say that I have read all the submissions both years. Reviewing the stories, essays and poems of so many talented writers is my favorite part of the process and improves my own writing.

I just finished compiling all of the contributors' bios, and I am once again awed by the diversity, experience and accomplishments of our *Well Versed* contributors. If you haven't done so before, read the Author Bios in the back of this edition, and get to know your fellow writers and guild members. I think you'll be both surprised and impressed. Every writer needs other writers who will give honest feedback, encouragement and comradery. I am committed to connecting the names in this book with the faces I see at our monthly meetings, and I hope others will do this as well (if you aren't already). Building relationships between writers is, I think, one of the most important roles the guild can play.

Finally, I want to pass on the most profound thanks to Yolanda Ciolli of Compass Flower Press/AKA Publishing for the generous donation of her time and expertise in the formatting and printing of *Well Versed*. I could do this without her, but it would be more painful and less professional.

Sincerely,
Maggie Maginness

Fiction

Fiction Judge

Although not a superhero, C. David Milles does have a dual identity. He is a middle school teacher by day and a writer by night. He enjoys exploring the building blocks of stories, especially through the lens of the Hero's Journey.

He loves all things geeky: superheroes, video games, reading, and writing. His favorites include television shows like *Lost*, *Fringe*, and *Doctor Who*, and movies like *Jurassic Park*, *Indiana Jones*, *Lord of the Rings*, and *Back to the Future*.

First Place Fiction

The Phone Call

Adria Waters

. . . his lips were . . . what?

Hannah shoved her glasses up on her nose and leaned down over the screen.

. . . *the scent of his cologne . . . hugged . . . overwhelmed . . . smelled . . .*

Taking a deep breath, she rolled her head on her shoulders.

. . . *enveloped her as he turned to leave. She knew she would never see him again and she sighed as she closed her eyes and watched him walk away . . . wait . . . what?*

"She closed her eyes and watched him walk away?" Hannah shoved her laptop aside. The movement upset a glass of day old water, splashing her dirty shirt with droplets as it landed on the floor. She ticked an eyebrow up. It was the closest she'd gotten to a shower in days. Jasper, the gigantic ball of fluff she'd taken in last year, jettisoned out from under the threadbare couch, distracted for the moment from his project of clawing it apart from the inside out by the spreading puddle of water. He touched it with a paw and then turned accusing eyes in Hannah's direction.

She chuckled. "Come on. Let's go see what we can scrape up for dinner." Ignoring his half-hearted attempt to scratch her, she scooped him up and trudged to the kitchen, the bottoms of her bare feet pricked by stray pieces of cat litter scattered on the faded linoleum. She placed the cat on the counter and absently ran a hand through his orange fur as she considered the empty cabinets. "Noodles?" she asked, showing him the package. The plastic wrap crinkled as she looked at the expiration date. "Call 9-1-1 if I keel over after eating this, okay?"

Jasper stared at her over his squished-up nose. With a noncommittal meow, he nipped at her wrist and then jumped down off the counter.

Hannah moved the dishes stacked in the sink and began searching for a clean pot. The silence in her small apartment was broken by the sound of a phone ringing. The noise jolted her and she turned to look at the avocado green rotary dial dinosaur that clung to the wall by the window.

As she stared at it, it rang again, the sound setting her teeth on edge. She hadn't paid the phone bill, or any of the others for that matter, in months. Rubbing her tired eyes, she grabbed the receiver. "Hello?"

Silence.

Hannah listened for a moment then shook her head. As she took the phone from her ear, a voice crackled out at her. Hoarse and unfamiliar, it sent a shockwave down her spine. She placed the phone to her ear again.

"... *she knew she would never see him again, and she sighed as she closed her eyes, not able to bear the thought of watching him walk away. Away from the life they had built together, away from the child they had raised, away from the promise of a lifetime filled with happiness. She took a deep breath and forced herself to turn before she allowed her eyelids to lift* ... "

"Who is this?" Hannah's brow furrowed as she gripped the phone with two hands. "How do you know what I'm writing?"

"... *the man who had been* ... "

She cleared her throat. "Who is this?" she asked again, her voice coming out a strangled whisper.

"... *tears clouding her vision as his arms* ... "

Hannah pawed through the junk drawer until she found a worn pencil and pad of paper. Shoving the drawer closed with her hip, she started to transcribe the words pouring from the phone. Soon her hand cramped, though, and she let the receiver dangle from the phone, twisting slowly on its cord as she sprinted through the hallway to retrieve her laptop. She sat down on the floor and pulled her computer onto her crossed legs. Her fingers flew over the keyboard as the voice from the line droned on through the night.

The next morning, Jasper nudged her hand, knocking it from the keyboard. She awoke with a start and looked down at the screen. *The Divorcée's Hunger* stared back at her, the cursor blinking under the period after The End. She scrolled through the pages shaking her head in disbelief. Jasper nipped her toe.

"Fine. I'm up, I'm up." Hannah grunted as she stood, stretching her sore muscles. The receiver hung by its cord and she picked it up. "Hello?"

Silence.

Five years later, Hannah welcomed the reporter into her spacious kitchen, offering him a seat at the expansive marble table. "Hot tea? I have the most delightful Tienchi flower tea I've been dying to try."

He sat down in the chair she offered and pulled out his tablet, stylus poised above the screen. "Yes, please. It seems the Nolah Riley series has been very good to you these past few years."

Hannah turned and leaned against the counter, a faint smile playing upon her lips. She brushed a manicured toe through the plush cashmere rug at her feet. "Yes, she has." She brought the tea service to the table, the delicate china clinking lightly with the motion. Pouring two cups, she placed a cube of sugar in her own and then curled into a chair, drawing her knees up under her. As soon as she sat down, an orange ball of fluff lodged itself in her lap where it started purring.

"This is Jasper?"

Hannah ran a hand through the cat's fur and nodded. "He's been with me through it all." Her voice fell a notch. "Even when times were tough."

The reporter smiled. "Twelve books and seventy-two consecutive weeks on the USA Today bestsellers list, a series deal with HBO, and talks with Vera Wang about a Nolah Riley line of wedding dresses. It's hard to believe you were ever down on your luck."

"I've been very fortunate." She took a sip of tea and licked her lips.

The reporter leaned back in his chair and looked around the kitchen. "So, what's next for the great Hannah LeBlanche?"

She glanced toward the wall over his shoulder.

He followed her gaze then turned back to her. "Doesn't exactly go with the décor, does it?"

"That's what my interior designer said, but, well, I insisted it come with me." Hannah's lips twitched as she took another sip of tea.

The reported turned to look at the avocado green phone and ticked his eyebrow up. "But," he cocked his head to the side, "it's not even plugged in."

Adria Waters is the author of the Ghost Hunters Society series and has seen ghosts all her life. She loves exploring the paranormal and goes on ghost tours in every place she visits. When she's not hunting ghosts, she loves torturing her family with road trips across the country to see every single sightseeing opportunity in the United States. Adria lives in Missouri with her very patient husband, her not so patient son, two cats who insist that they are human, and various little spirits that pop up to say "hello" once in a while.

Second Place Fiction

Trout Fishing in Missouri

Rodnie McHugh

~A tribute to Richard Brautigan~

July in Missouri tends to be a lesson in the futility of mind over matter. As much as my mind tells me I'm cool, the rivers of perspiration flowing over my brow and dripping from my nose confirm it doesn't matter what I tell myself, it's hot and I'm uncomfortable. This particular July, however, abandoned the expected futility by turning unseasonably mild. To celebrate the phenomenon, I went camping.

I realize that some of you may immediately balk at such an idea. You are committed to the proposition that "roughing it" is defined in terms of checking into a Motel Six even if the light isn't burning.

If, however, you'd allow me to assert that the merits of camping are best experienced when it is combined with another critical ingredient I believe you just might be convinced of its value.

Camping is that Mecca of well-being wherein the throes of mechanistic productivity yield to the tranquility of verdant slopes, chirping birds and the smell of fresh coffee percolating on an open fire in the morning. The metaphysical exercise that best enables the disciple to achieve true serenity is, of course, trout fishing.

In my case, all this quietude of soul lay only a few hours away along the Meramec River, just outside the Holy City of Sullivan. And I was determined to partake of its sacred experience—there was only one hitch in my plan. If I were to arrive in time for the Ramadan of Trout, I'd have to use my thumb since I did not own a car!

Luckily for me, the Fates decreed that my destiny included a friend, a friend who just happened to own a car and who happened to be going my way. And to top it all off, when I told her of my spiritual quest, she not only offered to be my conveyance but asked to join me in my pilgrimage. I jumped at the opportunity set before me and readily availed myself of both the ride and her company.

Early the following Wednesday at our prearranged time of departure, Becky swung by my brownstone flat and revved her engine. She was ready to go and so was I. I hopped down the two flights of stairs lugging my Martin

D-35, a borrowed sleeping bag and an over-used pup tent through the narrow corridors leading to the back entrance. Reaching the landing safely, I flung the door open and stepped into the parking lot panting like a Saint Bernard. There she stood waiting for our trek to begin, her arms folded across her chest and the Omni idling impatiently, We quickly stowed my gear in the back end of her vehicle and headed for breakfast at Ernie's Palace of Coffee and Camaraderie; the perfect way to begin any spiritual quest!

An hour later, feeling fat and sassy, we were Sullivan bound.

Highway signs flashed by rhythmically like the regulated circulation of a sprinkling system (ch-ch-ch), marking our departure and refreshing our souls with the anticipation of our flies dancing upon the waters luring a trout to strike. All along the way one town waved us goodbye as another welcomed us, each bidding us to enjoy its abundance . . . but nothing could circumvent us from our mission. Undauntedly, we pursued our destination—Sullivan, Missouri.

By mid-afternoon, we topped the crest of a hill overlooking the Holy City. We pulled over to better admire the view as though it were a picture postcard declaring "Wish you were here!"—and, of course, we were.

Driving slowly through the town, we cast our eyes upon its bounty. A Five and Dime offered "Today's Special: Open Faced Turkey Sandwich with mashed potatoes and green beans," all for a buck-ten. We saw a few men clad in denim and chambray drinking beer outside Pete's Place . . . obviously a good source of information regarding local habits and liquid refreshment. The town even boasted an Army/Navy Store, which Becky said was a good omen as we might need a few supplies later. What we really needed right then was a place to obtain our victuals. And behold, as if by a miracle, there at the end of the block stood a Piggly Wiggly. We motored down and parked. Grabbing our shopping list, we hurried inside the store and traversed its golden tiled aisles in search of eggs, bread, dried spaghetti, a can of marinara sauce and the essential ingredient to well-being, red wine. Our purpose accomplished, the Omni headed for Meramec State Park.

Twelve miles down the road appeared the Park on our left. We rolled onto the gravel lane leading to the entrance. The closer we got, the more anxious we became. Our desire to begin our rejuvenation was peaking—We had spent the entire trip jabbering about what we planned to do the moment we arrived, and this postponement of our ambitions was disconcerting— Coming round a bend, we saw the ranger station sitting among a grove of cottonwoods a short distance away. Finally—at last—I thought it would never come—the gates of Ishtar appeared before us and celebration loomed in our hearts.

Payment paid, circle made, solitary spot spied; we parked, unloaded, set-up the tent, cooked our dinner and poured a glass of fermented grape juice. Becky and I sat on a picnic bench sipping our wine and staring starry-eyed towards the river. With dreams of battered fish dancing in our heads, we slept well that night.

The next morning found us awake and dressed at first light. While Becky gathered fire wood and conjured up the flames with a little help from her can of lighter fluid, I cracked open the food locker to prepare a quick breakfast. Scrambled eggs, rye toast and hot coffee broke our fast and nourished our bodies for the day ahead. In a word: We were set to go.

With tackle in hand, we approached the Temple of Trout. Sunlight sparkled like diamonds on the flowing waters of the Meramec. Pillows of white dotted the lapis lazuli firmament. Birds chirped as they flew by, wishing us well. The breeze was balmy. The day was ours.

Along the path I engaged in a conversation with a fellow celebrant headed our way. As we walked along listening, his words poured over us like ice water. His prophecy was disheartening. All hope was shattered like broken glass along the roadside. Becky and I shuddered in his wake. We stood facing each other, despair hanging on our minds like Spanish moss in a cemetery. Preparing to rent our clothes and sit on a dung heap casting the ashes of our dreams into the air, we prayed that this message was false. But the words of this piscator brought us face to face with the grim reality that trout, whether rainbow, cutthroat or golden, don't know about Sullivan, nor have they ever heard of the Meramec. Instead, they run desperately to Bennett Springs, where an eminent Confederate General from Big Sur is sometimes seen baiting his hook for unwary readers.

"P.S. Sorry I forgot to give you the mayonnaise."

Mr. McHugh was born in Los Angeles, California where he pursued his undergraduate education. After earning his B.A. he spent a decade in the work force before moving to Columbia in 1981, where he earned his M.A. in History from the University of Missouri-Columbia He stayed on at UMC for five years working in administration at Jesse Hall. By 1990, he found his niche teaching world history at Hickman High School. Since his retirement in 2014 he has written his first novel, and has been published in *Well Versed.*

Third Place Fiction

Who Knows Where the Flamingoes?

Frank Montagnino

We live in an area where the lots are rather large. Aside from the pain-in-the-ass factor of having to mow all that grass, we like the spaciousness. It's the main reason we paid more for our house than we would have for similarly sized and appointed homes in other areas. Our back deck looks out over a forest. No people back there, just squirrels and an occasional deer.

The forest wraps around one side of our house forming a leafy barrier between us and the neighbors on that side. That's one reason we don't know the people who live there. They moved in several months ago - a young couple, much younger than we old retirees. I met the woman one day when they first moved in. I was mowing my lawn near the lot line and she was carrying stuff into their house. It seemed like the neighborly thing to do so I shut off the mower and introduced myself - welcomed them to the neighborhood. She seemed nice enough. We haven't spoken since. We wave when we see each other, but our schedules are so different that seldom happens. I've never met the young man. They live next door, but they might as well live in another town. We're that close.

And then came the flamingo. Not a real one of course, one of those plastic flamingoes that were so popular a few years back. I was walking one of our hounds across the street from their home one day when I inadvertently got a peek into their back yard. There, in all its pink glory stood a single plastic flamingo, anchored on its wire legs near the back border of their property. The sight sort of tickled me. It had been so long since I saw a yard flamingo I was certain that fad had gone out of style. Plus, it seemed so incongruous in the yard of people who own a motorcycle and a jeep.

At supper that night I mentioned to my wife that I'd spotted a flamingo in the neighbor's yard. She agreed it was rather amusing and we went on talking about other things. But somehow, I couldn't get the damned flamingo out of my mind.

"You know, we've got a bunch of them in the basement," I said, interrupting her in mid-monologue to which I wasn't listening because I was thinking about flamingos.

"A bunch of what in our basement?"

"Flamingos. You remember a couple of years ago when you bought a bunch of plastic flamingoes and we put them out back for laughs."

"I remember," she nodded. "We still have them? We've got to start getting rid of things."

The plan formed right then—between bites of meatloaf and mashed potatoes.

"You know what would be fun?" I queried.

"What?"

"I could sneak over there one day when they're both gone and put in another one."

Her smile got wider and I could tell she was imagining how the neighbors might react.

"I bet they wouldn't even notice the first one for a couple of days," she mused. "Then one morning over coffee the woman would be looking out the window and she'd ask the guy, 'did you put another flamingo out in the yard?' And he'd say, 'No. Why do you ask?' And she'd say because there's two of them out there right now."

We were both grinning like idiots by then, imagining what the neighbors might be thinking and saying.

"Of course, we might never know for sure since we never talk to them," I reasoned. "And even if we did, we couldn't very well bring up the subject without tipping them off that we were the guilty parties."

"That's true," she agreed. "But let's do it anyway. If nothing else, we'll get rid of those flamingos in the basement."

A couple of days later I waited until both their cars were gone and then I skulked around the forest between our houses, darted into their backyard and planted another flamingo next to theirs. I made it back home without being spotted or setting off any alarms.

Over the course of about a month, I'd planted three flamingos in their yard. Surely, they'd noticed the growing flock. Probably they'd wondered who the hell was cluttering up their yard. I suppose, given our proximity, my wife and I had come under suspicion. They couldn't have been annoyed by our little prank because I noticed during my doggie walks that the herd was still back there in the yard.

It was during my next incursion that it all went sideways. The exercise was now a month and a half old and frankly, I was beginning to tire of it. I only had two flamingos left so I decided to plant them both at once and be done with it.

My plan this time was to put the last two birds in a line approaching their house. In my mind, I could see the neighbors looking out their window in wonder as the flock of flamingos seemed to be advancing, eerily and somewhat menacingly toward them. I admit, I was over-imagining the whole escapade.

16

At any rate, I waited until two in the afternoon, my customary raid time, then, armed with my last two birds, I snuck around the forest and into their yard. I kept close to the side of their house, edging along with my back to the siding. There were no windows along that side. When I got to the rear of the house I peered around the corner. The coast was clear as usual. I assumed a half-crouch (for some reason) and moving quickly I slunk halfway past their deck and then angled out into the yard toward the cluster of pink. Three-quarters of the way to the herd I stopped and stabbed the wire legs of one of the flamingos into the turf - making sure the bird was facing directly at the house. Before I could turn to plant my last flamingo several steps closer to their deck, I heard a sound that froze me in my stupid crouch.

I don't know anything about guns, but I've seen enough movies and TV cop shows to recognize the sound of a pump action shotgun slide. I straightened up and turned around to face the house (and the music,) the lone remaining flamingo still in hand.

My neighbor was standing on his deck which was about five steps higher than the ground, so I had to look up at him. It was the first time I'd ever seen him close-up. He was a wiry guy with a grunge beard, wearing a camo wife-beater. He had a few tattoos, but I couldn't say what they depicted because my eyes were locked on the shotgun he had cradled in his arm and casually pointed in my general direction.

"We thought it was you," he said. His voice was flat, expressionless.

Embarrassed at being caught pink-handed, I chuckled and put my hands up in mock surrender. Although I hadn't imagined guns being involved, I had always known there was a chance I'd be apprehended in mid-raid. That was part of the fun.

"Busted," I said with a chuckle. "And guilty as charged."

He didn't reply, in fact didn't even crack a smile, so I went on. "Kind of strange to meet this way, I guess. My name is Frank. I live next door." I dropped my hands and started walking toward the steps leading up to his deck.

"Hold it right there," he said, and he swung the barrel of the shotgun so it was now pointing directly at my feet. "You're trespassing on my property."

"Trespassing? That's a bit harsh, " I protested. Involuntarily, my hands had risen to about shoulder height. My stance was somewhere between 'wait a minute' and 'hands up' except that one of them still clutched a pink flamingo. "We saw your one flamingo and just thought adding more of them would be a fun thing to do. Apparently, you don't agree."

"Trespassing and littering," he said, ignoring my friendly explanation.

"Littering," I echoed incredulously. "Well look, I'll just take them all back and we'll forget the whole thing." I started to turn to gather up my flamingos.

"Uh uh. I told you not to move. Just stay where you are."

He was balancing the gun in the crook of his left arm and with his right hand he pushed down a bit on the stock so the barrel rose until it was pointed right at my chest. The bore openings looked as big as saucers.

"Look, _____ ." I'd intended to call him by name, but I didn't know it, so I stumbled ahead. "This is ridiculous. My wife and I thought it would be funny to sneak over here and add to your single flamingo. You know - just to imagine what you two might be thinking. We certainly didn't mean any harm. Obviously, you don't think our little prank was funny, so I apologize. Let me gather up the birds and get out of your yard and we can put the whole thing behind us. No harm, no foul. And for sure, no need for that!" I pointed at his shotgun. Unfortunately, without thinking, I did it with the hand holding the flamingo.

"Hold it!" He tightened his grip on the gun. "Are you threatening me with that?"

I couldn't believe this asshole, motorcycle-riding, jeep-owning redneck was serious. "What!" I exploded. "Threaten a man holding a shotgun with a plastic flamingo?"

"It'll be a claw hammer in your dead hand by the time the cops get here."

This shithead meant it, I realized. And suddenly I was breaking out in sweat even though it wasn't particularly hot.

"You can't be serious," I mumbled lamely. "You wouldn't shoot someone over something as silly as this." I gestured behind me to the flock of silent, pink witnesses.

"You ever heard of 'Stand Your Ground'?"

My mind was whirling, and it took me a few seconds to realize he really wanted an answer.

"Stand Your Ground?" I repeated. "Yeah, I've heard of it."

"Then you know I'm within my rights to shoot you right where you stand."

"Oh no," I interrupted. "I'm not breaking into your home. I'm not threatening you with bodily harm. Stand Your Ground doesn't apply."

"You a lawyer?"

"No, I'm not a lawyer, but I read the papers."

"Well you're not reading the right ones. Thanks to this new administration and new Supreme Court, you don't have to be inside my home or even trying to break in for me to use deadly force to protect myself. If I'm afraid you're going to do me harm the law says I can shoot you. And as you can see," he went on without even a glimmer of humor, "I'm deathly afraid."

Jesus, I thought. This guy has researched it. He's just itching to shoot somebody—anybody—and I'm the one who just happens to be standing in front of him.

"Missouri hasn't passed 'Stand Your Ground' legislation," I croaked. I thought I'd seen that somewhere, but by now I was just stalling - hoping someone would come home or a phone would ring, or something!

"You're right about that," he nodded. "But with our new machine-gun loving Governor and this being a red state through and through, you know what a jury would think. If it even comes to trial, which I doubt - I'll walk."

I couldn't come up with anything else to say, but my mind was churning. He's probably right, I thought. He'll walk.

There I stood, my hands up and still clutching that stupid pink flamingo when he raised the shotgun so it was pointing right at my face and slid his index finger into the trigger guard.

Frank Montagnino is a retired ad man blown out of New Orleans and into the clutches of the CCMWG by Hurricane Katrina. If you're reading this, it means his partly true story made it into the anthology. He hopes you enjoy it.

Anonymity

Jana Stephens

She was born in 1918, just a couple of months before her mother's favorite brother died of Spanish Flu in the big epidemic. Her earliest memory was that of wondering if her father knew her name; he usually called her Sis, but sometimes he called her Gal.

Her only sibling was a brother who was eight years older. When she was about nine, she began to notice cold tension between her brother and her father. One night she was jolted awake by her father's shout: "As long as you're living in my house, you'll do as I say!" She listened harder but she heard no response; her brother's answer was evident when morning came. He was gone when the household awoke at daylight. The girl didn't expect to notice his absence since he never had much to say, but the stillness around the table was somehow more profound. Her parents were mostly quiet about everything; if they said anything about their runaway son she didn't hear it.

Their house was gray and dreary; it was just like other farmhouses of that time and place. It wasn't insulated except for layers of newspapers glued to the walls. What light there was came from kerosene lamps; they smoked when wind hit them. Even when the windows were closed in winter, strong streams of wind pushed into the house from around the frames.

The house stayed fairly cold in winter despite fires burning in the big stove in the front room and the cook stove in the kitchen. When the girl was little she wondered why the stoves kept their heat so close. Why wouldn't they allow their heat to warm the house? She always meant to ask but time passed and eventually she saw the answer for herself.

One morning during a particularly hard winter when she was around eight, her bed had barely warmed when morning came. As was her custom, she stepped to the basin to wash her face. None of the farmhouses had running water in those days and so there was a white enameled washbasin in each bedroom. Something fragile shattered as her fingers pushed into the water. Her eyes opened wide in the still-dark morning—ice! She was shivering all over by time she finished splashing water on her face.

The summers were a different kind of torment, for it was then that food was preserved for winter: vegetables from the garden and apples and plums from the trees along with strawberries, blackberries, and huckleberries. Every day in summer, the cook stove was fired up for hours at a time and the little house was stifling with heat. When the girl was little, she had another question about stoves and heat during these scorching days. Why wasn't the cook stove this hot in the winter? Somehow, it had become her practice not to ask questions. Her parents were busy enough without her pestering them.

As long as the girl could remember, she had helped prepare the vegetables and fruits for canning—she shucked endless ears of corn, she peeled apples and cut away bad places, she cored and then cut up tomatoes while her mother was at the stove getting food into jars. The only breaks were for cooking breakfast and dinner. Extra was cooked for dinner and whatever was left was eaten cold for supper.

When she was nine, her mother told her she was old enough to do some of the actual canning work around the stove. The girl had a towel to wipe her face but sweat made tickling paths as it ran down her belly. She felt bristly inside, but she tried not to think about it. Canning was just part of life if you were going to eat in winter.

The worst of all was the making of tomato ketchup; she perched on the milk stool over the enormous pot. If she didn't stir fast enough with the great long wooden paddle, red bubbles would form on the surface of the ketchup. Then they exploded. The explosions sent out missiles that burnt wherever they landed on her skin. They were worse than hornets. If she stopped stirring to wipe at the burn, the hateful ketchup would spew out not just two or three, but clusters of burning bubbles.

The next morning, the red spots on her hands and arms would be raw; her arms would ache from stirring, but there would be more tomatoes to be made into ketchup. Finally they would move on to canning heaps of whatever ripened next. pass

The days went by, and with them the years. The girl passed her thirteenth birthday and sometimes she wanted to scream out her name to her father. Would she never hear him say it? One August day while she and her mother were making ketchup, her father came in from the fields at noon and cleaned up at the washbasin for dinner. Then he said, "Sis, I see dinner's not ready." Something inside her broke open and for the first time in her life she talked back. She said, "My name is Ellen! Why won't you ever say it?" She snapped her mouth shut. She couldn't believe such words had burst from her.

Her father didn't say anything, just looked at her with his icy blue eyes while she stood on the milk stool and used both arms to stir with the long paddle. She had stopped stirring as she said those words to her father and now the surface of the ketchup was covered with exploding craters.

In about forty more years her father died of pneumonia. He had become an old man, spindly and frail. A couple of weeks after the funeral, Ellen and her mother were packing up his things when Ellen suddenly felt a catch in her throat. Her father was gone forever. The catch stayed in her throat all day and most of the next. Her father was dead. She had never heard him say her name.

At Alice's

Von Pittman

Arlo Guthrie's talking blues song, "Alice's Restaurant" got much of the country laughing back in 1967. But I didn't laugh then; I don't laugh at it now. I still remember another 1967 encounter at another restaurant named Alice's. It wasn't funny.

In my second year at Eastern State University, in Capital City, I was a dormitory proctor, now an archaic job. Nowadays, "residence assistants" work not in dormitories, but in "residence halls," for the stated purpose of assisting freshmen through "post-adolescent developmental tasks." In the 1960s, our entire job was to maintain a modicum of peace and quiet in the dorms for about twelve hours a day. It was a formidable—and largely futile—task. We also had the unofficial—but frequent and unpleasant—job of intervening in town-gown disputes.

Early on a spring Saturday afternoon Alan, a good friend and the head proctor in Griggs Hall, walked into my room. He reached over to my radio and turned off the Atlanta Braves game without asking permission. "Something up?" I said.

"You know Chris, the guy in the room to my left? He called me from downtown. He's trapped in Alice's with three other freshmen."

"What do you mean, 'trapped'?" I knew Chris, a bright blond kid from Avalon, New Jersey. He had been nothing but trouble since arriving in Capital City as a freshman. Like a lot of northern students, he didn't understand—or give a damn about—southern manners and conventions. He constantly shot off his mouth about how ignorant and backwards southern people were. And of course he wasn't all wrong; he encountered abundant examples of each. But he couldn't seem to understand that insulting the local people, especially while downtown or off-campus, was a sure way to get his ass kicked. He had only narrowly avoided real trouble several times.

Alan sighed. "He and his friends were trying to top each other telling redneck stories."

"And they chose Alice's to do this in? Why there, of all places? Not only is it a greasy fried chicken, overcooked greens, and sweetened tea place, it's always full of rednecks looking for a fight."

Alan rolled his eyes. "Who knows?"

"So what has that noble son of the Jersey Shore done?"

He reached for my pack of L&Ms, shook one out, and lit it. At least he used his own matches for a change. "Chris and his friends must have gotten a little enthusiastic in their descriptions of some of our local folks. Apparently words like 'shit kickers' and 'peckerwoods' were bandied about. Four guys at a nearby table just happened to be genuine peckerwoods, and apparently proud of it. One of them got all red in the face and said, 'I've had just about enough bullshit from you assholes. The four of you together couldn't change a tire if your damn lives depended on it.' One, in a cool, low voice, said, 'you boys ever heard of the Ku Klux Klan?'"

"Oh Hell!" This scared me. While rednecks are often unpleasant—even belligerent—the Ku Klux Klan is extremely violent. Even our students from New Jersey knew that.

Alan continued. "The cool customer, their obvious leader, told our students to finish their dinners, and said, 'Then we can all go outside and talk about manners. You pissants need to learn how to behave.'"

"Obviously we failed to teach them proper manners," I said sarcastically.

"Obviously," said Alan. "But it got worse. The apparent lead Kluker opened up his hand to show Chris a small box cutter, the kind with a single-edge razor blade. According to Chris, he snapped his knife open with a nasty 'snick' and held it against the outside of his leg. Because of the numerous people in the place, Chris was able to get to the pay phone and call me."

"Shouldn't we just call the cops?" This was not a fight I wanted any part of.

"Depending on who we got, that might not turn out too well," said Alan. "Undersheriff Hawk can be downright unpredictable. He might just put a lid on everything, or he might decide it would be fun to lock up a few ill-mannered northern students. Best we not take a chance with Undersheriff Hawk."

Alan had a point. "I guess you're right," I said. "Sounds risky. But if we can get two other guys, that would make eight of us against four of them. Who else is around this afternoon?"

Alan said, "Chuck's in the office. If Kent's in his room, that ought to give us enough." Neither Chuck nor Kent turned us down, although both looked as if they'd like to. We got into Alan's ancient Buick for the short drive—less than five blocks—to Alice's, on the east end of Broadway.

"We'll go directly to our boys' table, then walk and talk them out. Once we get our guys moving, we won't stop. We may have to slow down, but we've got to keep moving. And that will be even more important once we get to the sidewalk. If you have to talk to any of the Klukers, smile and be polite. We'll say we are taking our smartasses over to Dean Boggs, who is waiting in his office, ready to introduce our boys to southern manners, and probably itching to hand out some punishment. But we keep moving until they are in the car and I can back out. Then the three of you can walk over to the Fain Hall parking lot and I'll meet you there."

Inside Alice's the geography looked bad for us. Chris and his friends were at a table in a back corner of the dining room. All were pale. Closer to the front door sat three men with deep tans. One sported jeans and a sweatshirt; two wore bib overalls. A fourth man, in khaki work clothes, leaned on the back wall, next to the pay phone, making sure none of the students could get to it again. We walked back to the table with our freshmen.

"Have you paid your tab?" Alan asked. They nodded in the affirmative.

"Leave a bigger tip," I said, hoping that a show of respect for the hard-working waitress might help mollify, or even impress, the Klansmen who, no doubt, were working men themselves. The four scared students pulled out a few limp singles and added them to the pile of coins in the middle of the table.

As soon as the freshmen stood up, the table of offended southern gentlemen rose quickly and walked toward us. "These boys need a little learning," said the smallest of them, the man in jeans, who looked more like a ferret than anyone I had ever encountered.

"We're from Dean Boggs's office," Alan said. "The campus police called and asked us to get this bunch out of here so they wouldn't have to get involved. They said they'd rather avoid real trouble." Alan said. We pulled out our flimsy pasteboard ID cards. Nobody examined them.

"Did these boys sass you?" I asked.

"Damn straight," said Ferret-face, obviously their leader.

"We try to teach them good manners, but they're slow learners," I said. "We're about to take these boys over for a talk with Dean Boggs. He'll hand out some pretty tough punishment—or he may just throw them out of the university outright. He doesn't like these snot-nosed northern kids coming down and insulting our people."

William Boggs was the last of the old school, kick-ass deans of men in big southern universities. He was also the only dean who frequently cited from Greek in his speeches. Everybody in town knew him, or knew of him. To the old-time residents of Capital City he was seen as the last line of defense against the growing crowd of northern undergraduates changing the nature of our community and campus. But in reality, he knew times were changing and he actually helped lead the way.

We got our boys up and moving and kept them moving. Ferret-face said, "These boys was really asking for it." He, too, showed us a box cutter. But we kept moving. As we exited the building we heard two more box cutter "snicks." Once we got out the door and onto the sidewalk, the Klan moved in even closer. Their language coarsened.

Alan and I kept up our defenders of the Old South jive act. "It's no damn fun having to ride herd on ignorant Yankees who just don't understand southern ways—especially manners," we whined to the Klansmen.

Fortunately, the sidewalk was open to view and people were within eyeshot from three directions. Alan opened his car. We shielded the freshmen and pushed them into it. "We'll meet you at Dean Boggs's office," I said. Alan backed out into traffic and headed for the building known as the Academic Building, although no class had been taught there in well over a century. The students knew the threatened visit to Dean Boggs's office was a bluff. I'm pretty sure the Kluckers were at least ninety percent sure it was a scam. They might have been ignorant, but they weren't stupid. This kind of incident was all part of a sort of continuing town-gown kabuki dance which had been going on since at least 1960, and would continue several decades longer.

Kent, Chuck, and I headed across Broadway, onto the campus, then to the parking lot behind Fain Hall. By then Alan was there. He let the four freshmen out, told them not to patronize Alice's for a couple of years, and to go somewhere quiet and relax. That was good advice for us, too. We were all still shaking.

"Well, our boys learned something about life in the South today," I said.

"Yeah," Alan said after a long drag on the Marlboro he had bummed from Chuck. "And it's a damned shame."

I never did learn to enjoy Arlo Guthrie's rendition of "Alice's Restaurant." I never ate another greasy piece of chicken in Alice's.

Home Schooling

Kit Salter

Jake moved a lot as a child. Toward the end of a summer in the early 1950s, his mother decided that the two of them ought to move to Lexington, Kentucky. She had no kin there but she had once taught at a small college in the Bluegrass State and thought it would be a good place to try again. She also had a thing about Henry Clay. She wanted to live in his world for a while to learn what had made him such a great patriot.

Jake's oldest sister had a classic Packard convertible with a rumble seat. Mother, Maggie—the daughter with the Packard—and Jake loaded all the household stuff they could into the back seat of the small car. Jake was given the rumble seat surrounded by boxes that wouldn't fly away. The trio drove from the college town of Madison toward Lexington. Maggie was the only driver.

On the outskirts of Lexington, Maggie slowed her driving pace while traveling along a quiet stretch of highway with farm homes set back from the road and surrounded with groves of substantial trees. Suddenly she spotted a homemade sign saying, "Home for Rent." We could all see that it had porches on two sides, an upstairs, a gravel driveway, and a barn. Maggie pulled off to the side of the road, and turned to her mother. "How does this place look to you?" Mother, who had always loved trees and farms—but had not lived in such a setting for decades—replied with a nice grin on her face. "Do you think they'll rent it to us?"

A wide smile of relief spread across Maggie's tired face. "Let's back up and give it a shot."

Jake's sister turned the Packard around and drove up the gravel driveway. There was a sign taped on the kitchen door that said, "See J. R. Hicks across the highway for questions about rental. It has only been empty for about a month."

"Perfect," said Maggie. "Let me go and find Farmer Hicks." Mother and Jake got out of the car, stretched their legs and looked around. Maggie drove across the highway up a driveway toward another, nicer farmhouse.

As the oldest and the youngest studied the scene, they saw a big kitchen garden planted in the back of the house. There was also a small pen beside the barn that had some lambs and ewes eating from a broken bale of hay. But, the real crop scene was acres of massive fields of tobacco in full growth. Jake was impressed with how much his Mother seemed to like this place with only a ten minute exposure to it before Maggie returned-- with a look of joy on her face.

"We've got it! Farmer Hicks and I worked out a rent of $45 a month as long as we don't bring another bunch of people in to share it with us." Looking affectionately at her mother, she continued. "J.R. says you can garden to your heart's content, Mother, and Jake, you might even be able to learn some farming stuff and earn a little money by helping J.R. with some of the chores on this new farmland he's just bought."

In good spirits—and undertaking a process Mother and Jake had repeated many times before—the trio unloaded and moved what stuff they had brought with them into the no-longer abandoned farmhouse. There was a neat fireplace in the living room, a wood-burning stove in the kitchen, and three upstairs rooms in addition to the two downstairs bedrooms. There was a bathroom downstairs, too. Their luck was good because scattered through the house was a lot of furniture that had been left when the earlier owners had taken their money and moved to Lexington. In a few days, Jake's mother had made, yet again, a new world in a new setting to accommodate new life and fresh experiences for the both of them.

After a few days J.R. stopped in and told Jake's mother that he was driving into Lexington in the morning and would be glad to drop the two of them off at the school Jake would probably be assigned to. Maggie had already returned to Wisconsin for her job so Jake and his mother had no wheels. The offer of a direct trip was welcome news. Jake's mother decided not to go so Jake was picked up by J.R. the next morning and driven to a brand new consolidated elementary and junior high school.

Jake, after a good-bye clasp on the shoulder from J.R., was dropped off at the largest school he'd ever seen in his entire life. It was a universe of new brick buildings, each looking more ominous than the last. Jake breathed deeply then headed for the nearest doorway of what seemed to be the main building. Just inside the door, he asked a person he assumed was a teacher where new kids went for 6th grade.

"Go to your teacher's room."

"I don't have a teacher. I'm a new student."

"Oh . . . okay, go to the office. It's down the hall there," she said, pointing to a sign that said OFFICE over a door on the right. Jake went to that doorway, entered it and asked the lady at the counter who he should see about getting a sixth grade teacher.

She said, "Who have you been assigned to?"

"No one. We just moved to Kentucky."

"Where do you live? Why did you come to this school?"

"J.R. dropped me off here. He's a farmer who's a neighbor and said this was probably the place to go."

"Where are your parents?"

"My father's in the Philippines. My mother is at our place on the Fayetteville Road."

The lady had begun her responses in a somewhat curt manner but now seemed to see that this was more demanding than a regular student question. She nodded to another office lady to cover the counter for her. She wanted to get this curiosity squared away. "Well, young man, please come back to my desk. I'll need some identification and some money for book deposit." She put down her folder and asked, "What is your name?"

"Jake."

"I mean your full name."

"Oh, of course. I am Jake Hayden Cleveland." The 12 year old stood tall as he pronounced his formal and full name. The office lady caught her breath and sat a little more upright herself.

"Why isn't your mother here with you?"

"We don't have a car. And even if we did, she wouldn't be here. She doesn't know how to drive." There was a short pause. Jake continued. "I don't have any identification, but I know my birthday and stuff like that. I even know my mother's maiden name. And I don't have any money."

This rush of information made everything more intense.

"Of course you know your birthday. What I need is something that shows where you were born." Jake started to interrupt, ready to identify his birthplace but she stopped him.

"No, ...you're going to tell me that you know where you were born. I'm sure you know that but we need other information to get you into this school." Then quickly, "And you need to have papers and money."

"I have some paper at home, but I didn't bring it with me. I guess that was stupid. And we don't have any money. We are mostly living from our garden. I thought school was supposed to be free. Is Kentucky different?"

"Wait . . . . by papers I mean formal identification. We can maybe let that go until your mother can come in. And by money I mean $10.00 to pay for book rental. It's not even really a rental fee. It's to help cover replacement cost of books if you lose them."

"I won't lose them. Everyone in my family is reading all the time. All we do is read, except for my mother. Mostly she writes. But anyway I will take care of the books. And besides, we do not have $10.00." Jake pushed on to keep the office lady from ending the whole process because of a lack of funds. "J.R. said that maybe I could do some work on the farm and earn some money so if you can wait a while, I can try to bring the money in later." Then he added, "I don't know how Mother will get here. J.R.'s wife took her shopping once but that was on the weekend when she was off work. Are you or anyone here on Saturday?"

By this time, there were several heads tracking this whole interview. The office lady staked out new ground.

"Okay, Jake, here's what we'll do. I will write down 'Student Will Pay Later.' That will take care of the money issue for now. For the ID, we'll say that 'Mother is Not Available' today. That means we can go to the next step. I will assign you a teacher and put you in 6th grade and we'll see how it goes." She allowed herself a full grin and then said—as though she was speaking to the larger audience, "I've a feeling that you'll do just fine."

The helpful lady wrote out a few words on some papers and then looked up with a sense of relief. "Jake, go to Building 36 and see Mrs. Wilkie. She's a good teacher and is probably the best one for you to get started with. She will explain our system and rules." She looked pleased with herself as she edged the pages into a folder and gave the new 6th grader a nice smile. "How does that sound?"

"Building 36? Mrs. Wilkie? Okay. Thanks a lot. I will start saving money so that I can get the $10, but you don't need to worry. I won't lose the books."

Jake then left the office, walked down the hall, left by the door he had earlier entered and stepped out into the bright sunlight of a Kentucky August morning.

He spent the next twenty minutes looking for Building 36. He did not find it. His search was a little half-hearted because he was feeling bad about having zero dollars, no real identification, and not having a parent with him. "0h for 3" is how Jake scored the morning.

So after twenty minutes he decided to walk back three blocks to a set of railroad tracks that J.R. had pointed out an hour earlier, as they were approaching the massive school. He had told his young neighbor that those tracks ran right behind his farmhouse on the Fayetteville Road. He'd said that if Jake could not get a bus ride home, walking those tracks, in four or five miles, would take him right to the Hicks farm. J.R. said that Jake could cross his land, run across the Fayetteville Road, and be home.

Jake chose that solution to the morning's confusion. He did not go to school for that entire semester. J.R. gave him some jobs to do around the farmstead after Jake explained that he was a little ahead of the class at that big Lexington school so that it was okay to take a few months to learn some farming and earn some dollars. Jake said he'd go to school later. J. R. seemed okay with that. The boy worked three or four hours a day doing farm chores and helping with little jobs related to the tobacco harvest. He earned a dollar or two a day. He was proud to be a major source of cash income for the new Kentucky household that fall. Jake saw that fall semester as true 'home schooling.'

I Was Born

Rodnie McHugh

. . . on the hottest day in 1946. It was a Wednesday; the twelfth of August. The time was nine thirty-two a.m.. The Southern California sun beat down on everything in its path, leaving the vast population of the L.A. Basin desperately seeking relief from shade or breeze or any trace of water which had not yet evaporated. In short, it was a scorcher!

My father, an upholsterer by trade, had gone to work early that morning. He had just settled into his daily routine when the phone rang.

"Chet, it's for you."

My dad dropped what he was doing and took the call.

Sol, the shop's owner, kibitzed. When my father's voice cracked, he whispered, "What's wrong?"

"Elsie's at the hospital havin' our baby!"

"Jesus!" blurted Sol.

My father attempted to replace the receiver on the cradle to no avail. Fumbling with the black metallic object, he finally succeeded in laying it to rest on its perch.

"I gotta go."

"So go already! I got it!"

Chet put his supplies away and covered the chair.

"I'll call later with news!" he shouted on the run.

"Be careful!"

The twenty-three year old father-to-be dashed to his Model "A" convertible, hopped in, ground the gears and was out dodging cars on Olympic Blvd. as he made a bee-line to St. Mary's Hospital.

Morning traffic was busier than usual, and although he wanted to make record time, his better judgment won out and he slowed down . . . slightly.

Flitting back and forth between lanes, he passed one car after another until he came up short behind a street car letting off passengers at Western Avenue.

"Come on, come on," he muttered as an elderly lady slowly exited the conveyance.

Once the traffic was moving again, my father passed the trolley and proceeded as fast as congestion would allow. A mere five miles became ten as automobiles and green lights seemed to be against him.

Approaching Alvarado, he slowed down enough to make a swift left in front of two on-coming cars. A long honk cursed him from one, while the other brandished a hand gesture to convey his displeasure. Unaffected by either citizen, my dad continued onward.

There, up on the left, he could see St. Mary's sitting atop the 3rd Street hill.

Driving slowly along the hospital's frontage, he reconnoitered both sides of the street for a parking spot—nothing. He turned up a side street—nothing! Down Grant he glided—again, nothing. As his aggravation reached fever pitch, he noticed a car vacating a space less than a block away. He headed for it. Once in position, he backed in, slammed the door, and took off running up the hill towards his destination.

By the time he reached the entrance, my dad was a little worse for wear because of the heat.

Sweating profusely, he stopped to catch his breath. Somewhat collected, he stepped through the doors and asked the receptionist, "Where are the babies?"

A trifle confused, she queried, "What?"

My father didn't answer her. He turned pale instead, his eyes rolled back into his head and then he unceremoniously dropped to the floor'—At least the tile was cool.

Three nurses, standing nearby, bolted into action. In no time, they had the situation well in hand. Helping him into a wheelchair brought by an intern, the first nurse placed a cold compress on the back of his neck; the second gave him a sip of cool water; while the third held the wheelchair steady. This collective effort brought him back from the brink of enervation. Still looking a little pasty, his eyes blinked towards recovery.

"Going up!" announced the elevator captain.

The lead nurse managed to extract from my father the needed information. This accomplished, she and one of the others wheeled him to the lift. Almost immediately, they were transported to the fourth floor where they wheeled their patient to the maternity ward.

My mother, having come out of her drug induced sleep sufficiently to become active, took her cosmetic bag from the nightstand drawer. She brushed her hair and then rummaged for her lipstick and mirror. (Anyone who knew Elsie Gallagher knew that no experience, not even child birth, could ever prevent her from looking her best). She had just begun to put on her face when . . . .

Her attention was drawn to a man sitting in a wheelchair winged by two nurses. Through the dissipating mist of anesthetic grogginess she studied him, rubbed her eyes, and then, "Eureka!"

Fiction   33

"Chester Martin Gallagher, what the hell happened to you?"

My mother burst into laughter. Suddenly she stopped, grabbed her side and winced. After a pause, she resumed laughing, this time, less enthusiastically.

The other three residents of the room stifled a giggle when they beheld the sight. Even the nurses, who knew the back story, found humor in it.

My father timidly stated, "I ran up the hill and fainted. It's hot."

"Fainted from a little run?" chided my mother. "Well, Mr. Gallagher, I just gave birth to a ten-pound baby boy and you fainted from a little jog up a hill?"

If that wasn't enough, she pelted him with more laughter. The others subdued theirs completely. My father sat in the wheel chair, crimson faced and thoroughly mortified.

After the hysteria subsided and the room returned to some degree of normality, the ol' man wheeled himself over to my mother's bed. Rising from the chair, he leaned in and gave her a kiss.

"How did everything go, hun?"

Elsie began to answer when the doctor entered, clipboard under his arm and solemnity on his face.

"Good afternoon, Mr. and Mrs. Gallagher," he stated officiously. "I have something I need to discuss with you."

The doctor shot the wheelchair a puzzled look but said nothing.

In a half whisper, my mother asked, "What is it, doctor?"

My father scrutinized the spectacled man for any sign of what was to come.

Removing his glasses, the obstetrician stated matter-of-factly, "First, although your son's birth wasn't a difficult one, there were a few moments which caused us concern."

He had my parents' attention now.

"The attending nurse noticed that his color wasn't what it should have been, so upon finishing the delivery we examined him carefully. Having stabilized him, we placed him in an incubator to aid his intake of oxygen. Your son is what we call a 'blue baby', which simply means he has difficulty breathing."

My parents listened carefully to the narrative.

"We're keeping our eye on him for a day or so. Now what this means for you is we shall not be able to bring him to you for nursing. You'll be taken down to see him of course, but I must tell you, he's been placed on a formula."

My mother sank into her pillows.

The couple dreaded hearing anymore; but nothing could stop the doctor.

"In addition, during the delivery he received an injury to his collar bone which warranted our securing his left arm and shoulder to prevent any further damage."

My mother studied the doctor's eyes.

"There's more, isn't there?"

"Well . . . yes . . . there is."

Stumbling through the next few words, the doctor continued:

"We believe your son has an enlarged heart. Simply put, this means that the flow of blood is constricted which affects the flow of oxygen which in turn makes normal breathing difficult."

Before my parents could interject a question, the doctor droned on.

"Thus he's in the incubator until his breathing is normalized. We're hoping . . . I'm hoping this matter resolves itself before you're released."

"And if it doesn't?" inquired my father.

The doctor put his glasses on.

"Then we'll need to keep him a while longer. But we're confident that the problem should remedy itself within a reasonable period of time."

"And just what do you consider 'reasonable'?"

"I'd say no more than a few weeks at the outside. But as I mentioned, I believe he'll be ready to go by the time Mrs. Gallagher is discharged."

My dad nodded as if he understood.

What he did understand was the primary fact: I wasn't coming home anytime soon.

My mother fell silent. My father placed his hand on her shoulder.

"If there are no further questions . . . I'll check back tomorrow to see how you're doing, Mrs. Gallagher. And rest assured we'll keep you informed of how your son is doing."

My parents thanked the doctor, who nodded and exited, clipboard in hand.

The other residents of the room, having overheard the conversation, politely refrained from staring at the couple, even sympathetically.

My father moved the wheelchair out of the way. He stepped to the other side of the bed, slid a chair next to my mother, and sat down. He reached for her hand; she welcomed his. They sat for the longest time in silence.

The day for my mother's release came the following Sunday. My father showed up with flowers and enthusiasm. But as they waited for the nurse to bring the wheelchair, the doctor came through the door, clipboard in hand, looking like a harbinger of gloom.

"Well, hello, doctor," muttered my father.

Fiction   35

"Good morning, Mr. Gallagher, Mrs. Gallagher."

"Anything wrong?" queried my mother.

"Would you have a seat, Mr. Gallagher?"

"What is it now?" my mother quipped.

My father reached for her hand. She pushed it away.

"I explained to you the other day there was a chance we'd have to keep your son a while longer for observation."

Choosing her words carefully, my mother responded, "We know, doctor. But what is it now? And please get to the point! I don't think I can take much more."

A tear attempted an escape, but my mother's self-control refused it freedom. She glared at the doctor instead.

"Y-e-s. I'm . . . I'm coming to that, Mrs. Gallagher."

My parents held their breath.

"As you know, we've been studying your son's progress."

"Yes, doctor, we know!"

"We need to . . . ."

"His name is Michael."

"What?"

"Our son's name is Michael," stated my father, whose tone evidenced his loss of patience.

"Oh . . . yes, of course." The doctor blushed and then proceeded. "W-w-we'd like to keep Michael a few more days, perhaps longer."

The man in white moved his clipboard to his other arm.

My father chuckled under his breath, "Well, at least now I have time to finish his bassinette."

"Oh, for God's sake, Chester!"

"I realize this must be grating on you, but it is necessary. If it's any consolation you can contact the neonatal care desk night and day to check on Michael's condition. And I encourage you to visit him at any hour," interjected the doctor.

They tried to be grateful.

The doctor cut his losses and bid my parents goodbye.

A nurse entered as he left. She commenced to roll my mother towards the door with my father in tow.

"Care to see the little guy before ye leave?"

"Why yes we would, thank you."

The older nurse took them a flight up to the sanitized room where I was kept with two other babies who enjoyed similar accommodations.

My parents stayed about thirty minutes. Wishing they could hold me or stroke my brow, they placed their hands on the monitor's glass. To their surprise it felt warm. When they left, they gradually left by degrees.

Upon reaching the ground floor, my dad ran to get the car. My mom waited with the nurse.

In no time, the roadster appeared at the hospital entrance. My dad jumped out and helped my mother in, closed the door, thanked the nurse and got in the car. Kissing my mom on the cheek, he put the car in gear and drove towards home.

Eyeballing the rear view mirror occasionally, my dad watched St. Mary's getting smaller and smaller by the second. He thought of me lying within a machine in a sanitized room among strangers and hoped the days of our separation would be few.

Lost in Kansas City

Jana Stephens

Ellen sits on the bed in her five-dollar-a-week room in Kansas City, thumbing through a Photoplay magazine. The room is quiet this morning; there's not much traffic on the street below. It's the end of the month and everybody's low on gas coupons. The February sun struggles its way through the dingy lace curtains, and the radio's smooth voice says it looks like Hitler will surrender within just a more few months.

She thinks of the phone call and her stomach drops a little. She'll make it later. There's plenty of time. She turns a page, lights a cigarette. The cracked mirror on the wall reflects the smoke as it drifts toward the yellowed ceiling.

The news ends and the music resumes. Chattanooga Choo-Choo. Glen Miller. His plane disappeared before Christmas and they're still playing his music a lot; still talking some about the tragedy.

She stands and gazes into the cloudy mirror. Delicately sculpted cheekbones and nose, uniquely colored eyes. Bluish-gray. Since she was sixteen, men have looked her over. She fluffs her chestnut-colored hair into easy waves. The cigarette hangs from the corner of her mouth and she squints one eye against the smoke.

Ellen unplugs the percolator and pours a mug of reheated coffee. Sits down at the small table, crosses her legs. Her foot dances to the music, and she picks up the Modern Screen magazine that came yesterday. She'll leaf through it a little, just to keep her mind off things. Then, the telephone call. There'll be no more putting it off.

She turns several pages and comes upon a two-page spread of pictures. She speaks to the young beauties that smile up at her. "I am prettier than every last one of you smug-looking starlets! You got the right breaks, that's all. Breaks is why you're there and I'm here! Beauty don't get a girl a damn thing in this world!"

She turns a couple of pages quickly, but then stops and speaks again. "Well la-de-da! Bacall and Bogart! You've decided to get married!" She drops the cigarette into last night's empty beer can. The sizzle is familiar.

"Lauren, you look like the cat that ate the canary! And here I am: kids farmed out to my folks, working in this God-awful city as a cocktail waitress. Scrimping and still barely sending anything home on Saturdays! Well, Lauren, you're welcome to the old fart. He could be your dad, for God's sake!"

A photo of three small children—the oldest is four—hangs on the wall above the uneven heap of magazines. How will she ever put a roof over their heads, or even feed them?

Twenty-seven years old, second marriage gone to hell. The jerk drinks like a fish. Won't hold a job. Big hero joins the damn Army, getting shot at in Germany for the last six months. Her full lips become a clenched line as she snuffs the cigarette with assaulting blows. The short leg of the table thumps against the worn linoleum.

Smoking usually helps her nerves, but not today, not with that telephone call hanging over her head. She lights another, and the radio flashes into her consciousness. Duke Ellington. Cottontail.

He could get killed. Her stomach clenches and the lively tune tumbles into oblivion. The widow's settlement from the army would buy a little house outright. With that taken care of, maybe she could provide for her children. How kind everybody would be to a war widow with three little ones! People would want to help, want to protect her and the children. Things wouldn't be dog-eat-dog any longer.

The children. She thought she could make enough money to rent a place and move them here. "What a damn joke that was! What a chump!" She only lets her face crumple a little. If she starts crying, she might not ever stop.

Of course, without the kids here, she did have some fun for a while with the city fellows; so completely different than those two hicks she'd married. Kansas City men know how to treat a girl right.

The thought shoots itself into her head: the telephone call. She takes a deep breath and thoughts tumble over themselves. The radio—Benny Goodman. Sing Sing Sing. The best song ever. Ellen snaps the fingers of both hands, sways her upper body a little.

The light mood vanishes. Things might not ever go her way. It's getting hard to get rid of that idea, especially these last couple of weeks. She has to make that call. The forgotten cigarette smolders and forms another brown scar on the table edge.

Down in the street, a car horn honks and jerks Ellen from her thoughts. "In a minute. I'll go to the telephone in a minute. I could save my damn nickel; I already know what they'll tell me."

She plants her elbow near the edge of the wobbly table. The coffee is still a little warm. She takes a gulp and flips magazine pages, but pretty soon she takes a long drag and drops the butt into the beer can. She puts on lipstick, shrugs into a jacket.

She steps into the narrow hallway, darkish because one of the bulbs is burned out. The worn wooden stairs creak in all the places she knows they will. She walks out the door and the bright winter sunlight nearly blinds her for a few seconds.

She walks to the corner, slows sometimes to study her reflection in the shop windows. Gets to the pay phone, steps in. The folding door is resistant and emits a piercing squawk as she pushes it shut. The booth is stifling from the winter sun and the receiver stinks of cigar smoke.

All of a sudden she is nauseated. Takes some deep breaths, waits for it to let up. It's not nearly as bad as with the other three, at least not yet. She dials the number and finally the receptionist answers. Ellen drops in her nickel.

She had seen the doctor two weeks ago, gave a sample of urine. He told her to call back today. She waits for him to come on the line, waits for him to make it official. She bites her lower lip, hard. If she starts crying now, she'll never stop.

Too soon, the doctor's voice is in her ear. Jovial. "Congratulations!" he says, and she can't clench her eyelids tight enough to stop the tears that ooze through. Beauty don't get a girl a damn thing in this world.

Overheard on the Steps at Jesse

Cam Wheeler

"Yea, Mom, I'm doing well. My job is great so far. Nice people. Friendly. But, this continues to be such a weird place."

"---"

"No, nothing like that. Thankfully, no racism or sexual harassment. Well, lewd frat boys around town but that's not what's weird."

"---"

"Ummm, how can I describe it? There's so much . . . uh . . . stuff in code. It's like . . . maybe they use nicknames, or lingo, or maybe it's just me. I don't know how to say it."

"---"

"Some examples? Well, they call it COMO. This guy in my office, Miguel, asked me the first day how I like COMO. He was trying to be nice but when I said I hadn't been there yet, he laughed at me. It's taken me all week to figure out it's the town and not some restaurant or bar. But I still don't know why they call it that."

"---"

"Yea, I've tried googling it, but it doesn't help. And, at lunch yesterday, someone asked me where I'm from. When I said I grew up in a suburb of Boston, they all started doing it again—the code thing. Kesha said she's from Jeff. I wondered if she meant she's dating Jeff but he's married to Ashley, so I was afraid to ask. Then, Maria said she's from KC and I wondered, who or where or what is KC? David said he's from Harg, out in BOCOMO, whatever that means. And Rachel said she drives in from South BOCOMO. All I could think was, why did I take this job?"

"---"

"No, no, don't worry, I didn't quit my job. I thought about it but the job's fine. Better than fine. And the people are fine too . . . I guess. It's just this weirdness."

"---"

"Yea, I know, give it time. New places take time."

"---"

"I know. You've told me dozens of times about when you moved back east. But, really, this is making me miserable. Just when I think I can't get more confused, Dom says he's from The Lake. And I start to ask, 'THE lake. What lake is THE lake?' But I know if someone says, 'Lake Como,' I'm gonna have to be sedated. But instead, Jeff, the one married to Ashley, says he's from Cuba. And Ashley says she's from Lebanon."

"---"

"No, they aren't internationals, Mom. But, wait for it, it gets weirder. Josh says he lives in Mexico and commutes every day. And, Shelly, says, 'I almost forgot, I'm taking tomorrow morning off. I have to take my dad to the doctor in California, but I'll be here in time for the noon workshop.' I seriously thought I was being punked!"

"---"

"No, 'punked,' Mom. It means a group has gotten together and agreed to pull a practical joke on you."

"---"

"Yea, it's a thing people do. And someone videos it to post online for laughs and likes and shares."

"---"

"Exactly. They call it 'going viral.'"

"___"

"No. I'm not getting the flu. A virus is a type of computer attack that messes up your system. But, 'going viral' is when a video or meme gets watched or reposted millions of times."

"___"

"Yes, I know. I don't mean to confuse you. Anyway, I was totally convinced I was being made fun of, so I was trying to catch someone videoing with their phone. But they were all totally straight-faced. Just when I was about to demand they stop messing with me, Shelly starts crying because she thinks her dad's cancer is back. I felt like a jerk."

"___"

"No, I know, I'm not really a jerk. But, I almost acted like one. All because of the weirdness."

"___"

"Yea, it is weird, right? I mean, it's not just me."

"___"

"Oh, and by the way, they laugh when I say how glad I am to work for UM. For some reason, they call the University of Missouri, MU or Mizzou. Can someone tell me where that comes from? So, yea, nice people but some serious weirdness going on around here."

"___"

"No, I gotta go. I'll have to explain what a meme is when I call this weekend."

"___"

"Ugh, don't make me say it here!"

"___"

Fiction

"Because, I'm twenty-five and out of grad school and I just started my first real job."

"___"

"Ok, ok! Love you, Momma! Talk to you this weekend."

Click.

Route K

Kristian Wingo

The first thing people want to know about these kinds of things is whether or not there was alcohol involved. But there wasn't. Not really. It wasn't like I'd spent the night at a club with my sorority celebrating a 21ˢᵗ birthday. You know me. I'm thirty-six, a typical soccer mom with two kids. I was at our office Christmas party, for crying out loud. How boring is that? A bunch of parents with babysitters at home, meeting up at a friend's house to have a couple drinks.

Those opportunities are rare when you're a parent, trust me. And yes, some people got wasted. Brad had at least five shots, on top of all the beer he drank. If a cop had walked in there and breathalyzed everyone, only a handful of us would have been allowed to drive.

But I was fine. I'm sure I was. In the classes I had to take after I was pulled over a few years ago, we learned: "maximum four drinks for a guy, two for a chick." The night of the Christmas party, I only had a glass of Riesling with dinner and one of the shots Brad handed out. That's it.

So you see, it's not like I was careless. I'm a responsible person. I have to be. You can't raise two kids and perform at a job like mine without being responsible. Plus, I keep a nice home. We just got the bathrooms redone. I never let the dishes pile up, I dust twice a week. The first thing visitors always say when they walk in is how nice it smells. You want to know my secret? Two candles: one clean cotton, one cinnamon. Feel free to come over sometime. I'd love to have you.

Anyway, about that night. That's what you want to hear about, isn't it? There's really not much else to say. Jeff texted me to say that he'd put Josh and Alex to bed and asked when I'd be back. That was a good enough excuse for me to leave the party. I said goodbye to everybody and got in the car.

Rob's house is outside of town. You have to take these winding roads up and down hills to get there. There's not much light. It's pretty scary at night if you're not used to it. Pretty scary even if you are. There's not much you can do if you go around a tight turn and something jumps out in front of you.

I can't tell you exactly what I remember from the actual collision. It's not that I was drunk and blacked out or anything like that. I'm sure that's what some people would say. But like I explained already, I'd hardly had anything to drink. It's just that for some reason my mind didn't hold onto the memory of that moment. That's the truth. There's nothing I can do about that.

The same thing happened when I was eleven. My uncle fell off our roof and died. It happened right in front of me, but even the day after, I couldn't tell you what color shirt he was wearing or what the weather was like. It's just a quirk of my mind I guess. That night of the Christmas party, I only remember what happened after.

I pulled into our garage and checked the front of the car. I must have remembered hitting something at least. It was dented. There was blood on the hood. It's a white SUV, and the blood was just so bright against it, so bright that it looked like paint. Jeff must have heard me crying because he came out to the garage.

He said "Did you hit a deer or something?" He looked afraid too.

He brought out a bucket of water and soap. The blood came off easily. I was really worried about that.

The only thing left was the dent. Jeff pushed on the plastic around it to try to pop it out. He's a lawyer, not exactly a handyman. I'd never seen him work so hard, physically, at anything like that. By the time he gave up, he was sweating.

Jeff used to joke about my bad driving in front of our friends. I'd laugh, but it embarrassed me so much. I hated it. So when he couldn't get the dent out, the first thing I thought of was how it was going to be his new punchline. I imagined us at some restaurant with friends and him pointing out the window at the car. "There's the proof!" he'd say, and our friends would laugh. Pretty ridiculous, I know, given the circumstances. But that's what I thought about. Funnily enough, Jeff hasn't made fun of my driving since that night.

Somehow, the police learned that most of the people on the road that night had been at Rob's house for the party. They contacted Rob and asked him to get in touch with all of us. Rob sent an email to everyone who attended. He gave us the details: There had been a hit and run on Route K around eleven on the night of the party. The girl was walking home from her friend's house. According to the coroner's report, she had been killed on impact. She was fifteen.

In the email, Rob also asked if anyone had seen or heard anything on the way home. I wondered what he meant by that. A car on the side of the road? The body itself? Screeching tires? The bang of a skull against the car? I couldn't imagine what anyone would report.

Of course, no one reported anything. One of them could be lying, I thought. I went back to the night and imagined who it could be. Only Sharon and Tim left before me, so they were really the only potential culprits. Neither of them had much to drink and I didn't know either of them to be reckless drivers. But still, I imagined each of them driving on Route K, Sharon in her big SUV, Tim in his sedan. I imagined each of them ramming into the high school girl from behind, their headlights reflecting off her backpack in the second before her ponytailed head snapped back and hit the hood of their car. That could have happened, I thought.

Both of them replied to the email, expressing their sympathy but saying they hadn't seen anything. They could be lying, I thought. It could be a possibility.

The girl's name was Rachel Peterson. Her mom was persistent. She bought a big ad in the paper offering a reward for any information related to Rachel's death. When Jeff saw it, he said that those types of rewards are hardly ever paid out. If the police can't find the information on their own, it's very unlikely that a reward-hunting citizen can. It really only happens in movies. I asked him if we'd put out a reward if something like that happened to Josh or Alex. But, we told ourselves, nothing like that would ever happen to either of them. We'd never let them walk on that kind of a road at that time of night. I mean, would you let your kid walk around in the dark around speeding cars? Jeff said that Mrs. Peterson's reward reeked of guilt. She was guilty of bad parenting. I had to agree.

The reward ad came out on Christmas Eve. Everyone in the office said how sad it was. I had to agree with them too. Even bad parents shouldn't have to spend Christmas without their child.

But like I said, Rachel's mom was persistent. A few days after New Year's, she got the police to go around questioning the people who had been at the party. They stopped by Tim's house and he said they might stop by a few or our houses too. He said the cop had been apologetic. It was pretty clear that Mrs. Peterson had been pestering the police office incessantly. When I got home, I told Jeff and we made a plan for what I'd say. If they asked if I'd hit anything on the way home, I'd say no. Had I drunk anything? Just one glass of wine. And the dent? From a basketball, about a year ago. Kids, you know?

Then, sure enough, a day or two later, a cop car pulled into our driveway. It had been awhile since I'd talked to a police officer. There's nothing to worry about, I told myself, but he was still intimidating. The gun and the handcuffs right there on the belt. Even if you haven't done anything wrong, it's terrifying.

My mind just went blank, and a moment later, the rest of my life was playing out like a movie I had no control over.

The police officer told us there had been an accident on the night of Rob's party. He asked if I had been drinking. One glass, I said, like I practiced. He brought up my DUI. I said it happened years ago.

He asked if he could see the car. Jeff tried to stop him, but the cop had a warrant. Jeff would have objected if it wasn't lawful. He asked about the dent of course, and I recited the basketball story we had planned. The cop said it looked like it was caused by a human head.

He left. A day later, another cop came to the house, handcuffed me, and threw me in the back of his cruiser. I was questioned in the county jail.

We went to court. There were wall-size photos of my dented car for the jury to see. They heard about my DUI from a few years ago. Rachel's mom was in the courtroom.

I was sentenced to a year in prison, a light sentence based on the lack of evidence and great bargaining from the lawyers Jeff had hired.

Jeff brought Alex and Josh to visit me in jail. I wished they didn't come. Their mother was a criminal now. They lost their friends because parents didn't want their kids to be around our family.

I got out of prison. I lost my job and couldn't find another one. No one would hire a felon. I stayed at home. I spent all day making the house nice, but we never had guests. My boys grew older and they began to resent me. The kids at school teased them for what I did. Jeff and I divorced once they both went off to college.

None of that was as bad as the worst part. The worst part was that I knew what people said about me: "She killed someone." And technically, it wasn't a lie. But what do you think when you hear that? Cold-blooded murder, right? A gun or a knife or a push off a roof. You know I'm not that kind of person, right? But that's what they said: "She killed someone. She's a killer."

That's what flooded through my mind as the cop talked.

But in the end, none of it happened. I don't even remember what the cop asked us. We didn't open the garage door for him, didn't show him the dented car. After a few minutes, he just got back into his cruiser and drove away. We never heard anything else about the matter. It was all over just like that.

I've thought about that night a lot since then. I thought about how I could have stopped and checked. I could have called 911.

But then what? What would that have changed, really? Ruining my life wouldn't have brought Rachel back, right?

By the way, Alex and Josh are in college now. They're doing great. Come over some time and I'll show you some pictures.

Anyway, thank you so much. I just really needed to tell someone. And besides, it was probably just a deer.

Southern Discomfort

Kit Salter

Written in response to images created by author Von Pittman in his evocative depictions of cultural tensions in settings in a southern college town.

As Maggie got out of her fully unrestored 1967 Plymouth Fury, she saw three bunged up trucks parked in front of Lee's Place. She didn't recognize any of them, but seeing more trucks than cars gave her a pretty fair sense of the crowd she'd be serving this Thursday night. That was okay. There might even be a tipper in the truck crowd. The damn college Volvo kids hardly ever got beyond ten percent.

As she cinched her black apron around her still pretty good shape, she walked toward Lee's with the light step that the General favored in his help. Just before she entered the main door, she wondered again why his parents gave him the first name of 'General'. He was born on Peril Harbor Day 1941 and it was pretty clear that the Confederacy was not about to rise again.

General Lee's greeting was predictable. "Hey, Maggie . . . how come you took one of the best parking spots on the street? Ya know I'm always trying to keep those open for new customers."

"It looks to me as though you already got some new customers, General. They must be driving those trucks to the Demolition Derby this Sunday."

"Hold on, Maggie— those boys spend their money on beer and Bibles. They don't squander it on truck washes like some . . . "

"It'll take a helluva lot more than a truck wash to bring those bodies back," she quipped and then added, "but if you think my Fury's not going to bring in the sort of trade you want tonight, I'll move it across the street in front of the Golden Corral."

"Yeah . . . that's just the place to have it. It will jack up the heartbeat of the old folks walker-ing in to the buffet line."

Maggie grabbed her keys and went outside, unlocked her Fury, and did a big U Turn on Monument Street. She slipped into a spot ten feet from the competition's entrance. Ambling back toward Lee's, she looked to see if there were any cars with northern plates in front of the Place. A herd of local trucks and northern Volvos always made her a little uneasy during the night shift. Right now all she saw was an Ohio plate on a Camry. She went in and felt ready for—what?

As she wiped down the Formica counter she let her mind wander back to why she'd moved here in the first place. The town was clean and it did okay as a small college berg. The regional state university had a feisty football team and won just enough games to almost bring Town and Gown together on winning fall weekends. She admitted to herself she'd never seen any gowns in Lee's, but there were a lot of townies who fit right into the booths, around the tables, and at the counter. Because it was close to campus, General Lee could only sell beer and wine. That generally kept the lid on things.

At that moment, back in the corner of the Place, there were four guys who looked as though they must be the distinguished truck owners that Lee was welcoming. Maggie walked toward them, cinching her apron up just a little more as she came into their circle of conversation and smoke. "Hi, boys . . . it's time to get ready for real action now 'cause Maggie's here! What can I refill for you, or even add to your pretty piss poor range of things presently on your table? "

The first one to speak up was not the best looking of the quartet—the one that Maggie would have preferred bantering with—but the shortest. He was not quite pudgy. He was stocky and cocky.

"Well . . . we're sure as hell glad you're here, Maggie. We've all turned down drink and dinner options at the Country Club so we could come and get you to make sense of the evening." There was clear self-satisfaction in his presentation and Maggie returned it with a sharp "Welll, Carhartt, I bet the Club Ladies are weeping tonight because you opted for Lee's Place and not the swamp margins by the river. What can I get you to start the best part of your day?"

"Maggie. I'd like some foreign beer . . . say, a Schmidt's from St. Louis. Does the General buy such rare brews from so far away?"

" . . . and I'll have a really cold Bud—but NOT Bud Light." This was said by the good looker so Maggie was quick to say, "Wait, John Deere, . . . let me get my order book out so I can get the details of your every wish." She pulled a pen from her hair and wrote words in a small spiral bound notebook. "What else, gents?"

The other two men seemed to be cut from different cloth. One looked up and said, "I'm good." The fourth man just stayed quiet and gave Maggie a small nod.

Maggie replaced her pen, and headed back toward the Formica counter.

It was then that she noticed three college boys at a table that was somewhat hidden from the four truck guys. As she walked into their view, two of them raised their arms to wave her over.

"Damn . . . we thought we'd never get your attention. What do you have in the way of draft beers?" Maggie, always put off when people suggested she was slow in getting to their table pointed to a large chalkboard above the counter. "See where it says, 'DRAFT BEERS'? We often have several of those. Which one do you favor?" The fellow who had asked reached into his leather briefcase, probably searching for glasses. He found them, put them on and read the wall. "I'd like a draft Coors."

Hearing no Please, Maggie's next line was invariably, "Do you have an I.D. you can show me?" She asked exactly that.

The guy looked at the other two. "An I.D.? You mean to show that I am old enough to drink beer here?"

"That's it. I'm not conducting any Elections here. Just need to see proof of your drinking age."

The boy mumbled something as Maggie extended her hand to receive the I.D. He pulled out a leather wallet from his Khakis and extended it toward Maggie.

She put her hands up as though to stop action. "Like the cops, young man, pull the I.D. out. That's all I need to see. Don't want you thinking that I'm trolling for a Tenner to overlook any age deficiency."

The kid blushed a bit and fiddled with a tight compartment in the smooth leather billfold and then handed his Driver's License to Maggie. After a quick look, she said, "Okay . . . a draft Coors." Looking at the other two as they were freeing up their own I.D. cards, "What else, boys?"

"What's the least popular drink you have here?"

"The least popular?"

"Yeah . . . I want to buy something that none of these rednecks drinks." As Maggie heard this statement, she looked over her shoulder just enough to see that the truckers were more or less involved in their own conversation. They may or may not have heard this boy's selection process.

Maggie gave him her full attention. "Green tea is a slow mover. We could add pickled pigs feet." She had her pen poised over her notebook again.

"No . . . not pigs feet. Add a shot of Sam Adams . . . do you sell Sam Adams here?" Maggie kept her eye on him but pointed to the wall poster again. "Look over there. It begins with S. Do you see it?"

A pause. "No . . . but I do see Rainier, a nice mountain beer . . . it couldn't come from here. Add a shot of Rainier to my green tea . . . and how does a beer as unknown as Rainier find its way into Lee's Place, Missy?"

"Not Missy, mister, Maggie. General Lee is a big fan of Longmire, a TV character combining the smoothness of the South and the vigor of the High Plains. Probably not a world you've seen yet." The fellow was about to reply when the third guy said, "I'll have a Bud. I heard one of the boys over yonder ordered a Bud and that's a good sign. I'd like mine cold, too."

"Okay, fellows. A draft Coors, a cold Bud, and a green tea with a shot of Rainier beer. You know you'll have to buy the whole beer, right? Anything else?"

The first guy to order said, "No, we'll see how the drinks work out."

Maggie walked back to the counter, replacing the pen in her hair. She called out, "Green Tea for table 6."

The trio that Maggie thought might have a Volvo, laughed and the big guy said, "Do make that Oolong 'cause it's for me." They snickered and returned to their conversation. They were talking as though they were in their own dorm room.

"Think of growing up with this Main Street and town being your entire world. How'd you ever learn to talk to a city person or a banker, or someone in investments? How could you live your life looking backward to some mythic southern glory rather than getting ready for the real world ahead? How could you even talk to a doctor?"

"You'll wish for a doctor's office after your green tea, pigs feet and Rainier beer, halfass." This comment came over the top of the thin partition that separated the truckers from the college boys.

The college trio went silent.

The voice from afar got louder as chairs scraped the floor while the truckers stood up and walked around the partition. "The whole world is right here, yankee boys, even green tea. What you dorks don't seem to learn is that coming to a college town doesn't just mean classes, it means figuring out how the whole scene works."

The tea boy spoke up. "There's gotta be something besides shit-kicking demolition derbies and Bible thumping holy rollers to bring you into the present. You oughta be glad that men like us come from our world to give you boys a sense of what you're missing." By this time, the four truckers had surrounded the three college kids. The Volvo boys were still sitting at their table.

"Naaa . . . all we learn from you northern gasbags is that you can't drive a stick shift, you don't know shit about changing a flat tire, and you waltz into a place like Lee's just so you can think you're really cool."

Just as green tea was about to push back his chair and stand, Maggie swept in with a tray of drinks. "Okay boys, if you don't get back to where you all were 20 minutes ago, I'll never know who ordered what. Truckers, please return to your table. And," she gave a big smile to the short stocky one, "I've added a free plate of General Lee's Thursday Wings. Follow me and my tray around the corner."

Led by the smell of the wings and the moves of Maggie, the local boys followed. But as they turned the short one said, "If you boys want to understand the 'real world,' you've got to shake off Dad's money and look around you in a place just like Lee's. I bet Maggie could teach you a lot here."

The trio sat down without talking and in a minute Maggie returned with tea, Coors and a cold Bud . . . and part of a Rainier still in the can. There was also a basket of wings on her tray.

"Boys, I been in college towns since before you were born. I can tell you that real education begins way outside the frigging lecture room. I just saved your asses from a major lesson—and, believe me, your parents wouldn't have been interested in covering the costs of General Lee's furniture as part of your southern education."

Thin Ice

Susan E. Koenig

Thin ice. Figuratively, I knew I was skating on it with my satin shawl wrapped around me like I was some nineteen fifties movie star. If I still smoked, which is now considered unhealthy and unglamorous, I would have used one of those thin black cigarette holders to keep smoke from stinging my eyes.

I wiggled my satin sheathed butt all the way up the stairs to the new nightclub, the one all over the news, and batted my false eyelashes at the bouncer as I tried to sashay past. He shook his head like a man wondering how to humor his eccentric aunt. The red carnation tucked behind his name tag, which read Terrentino, reminded me of the way Johnny used to tuck a rosebud in his pocket before we went to a dance.

"How did you get up the stairs?" Terrentino asked.

"The same as anyone else."

He tried to engage me in a chat. Aiming to be sociable, I couldn't move past him, but I wanted to go into the party.

In my mind's eye, the women inside were wearing satin gowns with satin shawls like mine, except without the beautiful tiny pearls sewn on by my daughter when she borrowed it for her senior prom. I watched in alarm as partygoers walked past wearing everything from spandex to bikinis. No gowns, no satin. Mind-boggling.

My hunky bouncer lifted his lapel and said something I didn't quite catch, but two minutes later, another man dressed in a similar black suit and bow tie came along.

"What's going on?" He frowned as he spoke to Terrentino.

"I need a minute to help our friend here."

Terrentino, or Terry as I called him, offered me his arm. I had worried about not having an escort, so I was thrilled. The first time Johnny offered me his arm was the night we met at Club Trocadero in 1943. The band played "In the Mood," and was I ever. His friend snapped a picture of us, Johnny in his Navy uniform, me in my knee length burgundy velvet gown.

Instead of going inside, Terry surprised me with a walk down the ramp, not the stairs, to a bench a short distance from the circular drive where a cab had dropped me off earlier. As we chatted, I lied a little. I told him I had forgotten my invitation. He asked if it was back home with my white gloves. I told him yes before I realized he was putting me on. Humiliation burbled.

"Where do you live, ma'am? Over in Graceful Lake Retirement Village?"

"Oh, my word, no." Blood pounded in my ears. "I live in my own home. Why would I live anywhere else?"

"And where is your home?"

I thought it improper to tell him, so I said, "Not far."

"May I see your driver's license, Ma'am?"

I gasped. "You're carding me." I couldn't hide my pleasure as I searched my white beaded bag and pulled out my license.

His grin spread into deep dimples as he read it. "You're looking lovely tonight, Miss Lofton, young and lovely." He handed the license back.

"Please, call me Janie." I tucked it into my beaded bag.

He stood and I accepted his extended elbow.

When he signaled a cab waiting near the curb, I turned my most woeful, pleading eyes upon him. "I haven't had one single dance tonight." In fact, I hadn't had a single dance since the night a year ago when Johnny was still alive. He had been handsome as ever in a tux and I had worn my peach satin gown. We danced in the family room, our last dance.

Terry's eyebrow arched. He moved his arms into position as if he knew how to do a proper swing, but he didn't fool me. "One dance," he said. I placed my hand in his, which he pulled into a resting spot on his chest, like Johnny used to do. I felt a flood of warmth like the summer night on Fiji so many years ago when Johnny told me about his promotion and I told him we were going to have a baby.

We danced on the sidewalk, Terry and I, slowly rocking back and forth. "Happy birthday," he whispered. The dance ended and I realized we were standing next to the cab. He opened the door, bowed, and swept his arm toward the seat with a flourish of invitation while he recited my address to the driver.

I protested. "I want to go to the dance inside the building." To be honest, Terry was a good dancer, but I only ever wanted one dance partner, and he's gone.

Terry made a tsk, tsk, tsk sound with his tongue. "You have a nice evening now, ma'am." He helped me into the cab. "Take care of this beautiful shawl." He gathered the excess fabric so I could hold onto it while he closed the cab door.

He stood at the curb as the cab pulled away.

And so ended my ninety-ninth birthday splash.

Sunday Breakfast

Stephen Paul Sayers

Sunday after church, Melanie Maxwell rode in the station wagon's back seat, her father driving, her mother beside him. With their weekly religious obligations fulfilled, the family headed to Wurdig's diner out at the far end of Route K, home of the "belly-buster" breakfast. The little girl gazed through the side window at the world flying past, a rumble in her stomach, wondering why pancakes always tasted so much better after church. Other restaurants closer to town served a breakfast just as delicious as Wurdig's, but no one seemed to mind the extra miles together. One of Melanie's favorite games on their Sunday drives involved her mother or father pointing to a car and asking her to tell a story about it. Her imagination piqued, Melanie could weave quite a fantastic tale.

"So, where are they going?" Her father asked, nodding toward the ancient VW van crawling in front of them, a smattering of faded bumper stickers across its rear window.

"Hmmm . . . " Melanie chewed her lower lip, "actually they're not going anywhere. They're coming home."

"From where?" Her mother raised an eyebrow.

"Not where . . . when. They were caught in a time swirl."

"That sounds scary."

"It is!" The little girl leaned over the front seat. "They went out to breakfast thirty years ago and disappeared until just now."

"They must be hungry," her father offered.

"And thirsty, too," Melanie added.

Her father clutched the steering wheel tighter. "Probably why they're driving so slowly," he mumbled.

The little girl loved Sundays and time spent with her parents. She also loved the diner, the sound of plates and glasses clinking together, the bell dinging when an order came up or the cash register opened, and the din of cheery conversations filling the air. Melanie's order never changed—the silver dollar pancakes—always just the right size. Plus, since they came in a stack of twelve, she could eat all day and never come close to finishing them. Her dad would get the "belly buster" with extra bacon—every time—and pineapple juice. Her mother proved to be a mystery, though, always a surprise.

Today, Melanie and her mother played a different game once they arrived at the table. "Okay, honey," her mother said, "what am I getting for breakfast today?"

The little girl scrunched her face, trying to guess what her mother would order. "Let's see, you're getting the French toast . . . with cherry pie and a vanilla milkshake." She lifted her wide eyes to her mother.

"You're amazing, Melanie. That's exactly what I planned to order!" She gave a quick wink to her husband.

"I knew it."

"You know, Melanie, every day provides opportunity for new adventures. Eating the same food all the time makes life too predictable and boring." She said this while peering at her husband. He glanced up from his newspaper with mock irritation, just a quick peek over his glasses, making her mother smile and Melanie giggle.

The little girl loved Sundays.

After breakfast, Melanie's parents sipped their coffee and talked about grownup things while she colored on a paper children's menu. An uncomfortable dizziness fell upon her, darkness sweeping across her vision like moving clouds drawing shadows across a patch of lawn. She dropped her crayon and stared straight ahead, unseeing—the pictures playing in her mind, like a movie. A movie about her family.

Only the movie wasn't a happy one at all.

Blood spattered their faces, and her mother lay sprawled in the road with her head dented in and her neck bent backward. Her father's crumpled body rested on the car's hood, halfway in and halfway out the windshield, his legs bent in places they didn't normally bend. A gurgling sound bubbled from his throat as he tried to breathe, like when he blew milk bubbles with her through a straw at the kitchen table. No sound came from her mother. A big white truck, decorated with a picture of cows and milk bottles, rested way too close to the car, steam billowing from its engine. People stood everywhere watching them, covering their mouths with their hands, gasping. No one moved. They just watched them. In an instant, the movie in her mind stopped.

Melanie lifted her head. The restaurant sounds once again swelled in her ears. Her father gave her a wink as he dropped a handful of bills on the table.

"Okay, time to hit the road." He slid from the booth.

Melanie crept under the table instead.

"Melanie, honey, get off the floor." Her mother reached for her under the table. "It's dirty under there."

"We can't leave yet." The little girl pulled away from her mother, grasping the table leg.

"Honey, I told you last time, it's disrespectful to the people waiting to eat." He shrugged at the hungry family waiting for their table.

"We have to wait."

Her father folded his arms. "Melanie! Let's go!" Other patrons stared at them, shaking their heads.

Melanie closed her eyes to see if she could replay the movie in her head, but she saw nothing. It usually didn't take long for the pictures to go away; she just needed to wait a while. If she waited and still saw the pictures, she needed to wait longer.

"Okay, I'm ready." She crept from under the table and reached for her parents' hands, walking them outside the restaurant, across the gravel parking lot, and over to the car. Her mother and father exchanged a glance as they buckled their lap belts, whispering in hushed tones.

They eased into the heavy weekend traffic heading south on Route K. They drove for a few minutes until they approached the intersection of K and Highway 63. At a stoplight, her mother leaned over the backseat. "Hey Melanie, do you see the milk truck up ahead with the cows and bottles painted on the side of it? Tell us a story about that one."

This short story was adapted from a chapter in *A Taker of Morrows* by Stephen Paul Sayers (Hydra Publications, 2018). Available on Amazon.

Flash Fiction

Flash Fiction Judge

Over the summer of 2017, the Columbia Writer's Guild ran four "Fast Flash Fiction" contests. Each week guild members were emailed a picture as a writing prompt. Participants had 24 to 48 hours to write and email a response of no more than 200 words. The submissions were collected and then emailed to the guild membership as a group. Guild members voted for their favorites, results were tallied and later that week two to four finalists were announced. All of those  finalists and honorable mentions are included here and were sent on to our flash fiction judge Dr. Scott Dalrymple, who selected the overall winners.

Scott Dalrymple, Ph.D., the 17th president of Columbia College, has worked in higher education as a tenured professor, department chair, program director and dean. Dalrymple holds a doctorate and master's degrees in English and a master's degree in business administration from the University at Buffalo, as well as a bachelor's degree in English from the State University of New York at Geneseo.

Prior to his work in higher education, Dalrymple spent eight years in marketing, finance and entrepreneurship in corporate settings. He has published several books, peer-reviewed articles and pieces of fiction.

Dalrymple and his wife, Tina, who holds a doctorate in nursing and currently serves as Nursing Program development coordinator at the college, are both first-generation college students. They have five grown children and two grandchildren.

First Place Flash Fiction

From Week Three Contest

The Madman's Concerto

Kristian Wingo

The world expected another masterpiece from him. He hid in the basement with his typewriter to avoid the pressure.

In the silent isolation, words and ideas flowed. But then, when he read his writing again, nothing made sense. He pressed on, filling the empty house with tapping, getting nowhere.

At the end, he stopped buying paper. He hated the way the neat white blocks came down the stairs and turned into jagged, inked balls. So he typed without it.

His most beautiful stories, he was convinced, were written with dried ink on that canvas of air, vanishing each time a metal arm tapped the typebar. The music of his ephemeral literature delighted him. The world be damned.

Finally, as a grand finale to this private concerto, he stood up from his seat and smashed several keys at once, again and again. The tapping became crashes, until the tiny metal arms jammed together into a dark haystack and became silent. Satisfied, he wiped his brow, took a deep breath, and bowed to no one. He left his umbrella and went outside, where the raindrops clicked like his instrument.

His body was found a few days later. The typewriter remained silent.

Blue Silk

Ida Bettis Fogle

After he'd given her a light, the undulating smoke was like blue silk. It matched her dress. He'd never forget his first sight of her, the smooth, indigo fabric hugging her curves. The whole evening was blue silk—his tie, the jazz to which they danced, the night sky when they went walking later.

His two nieces believe something floral would be appropriate. They bring what looks like a Sunday school outfit for his approval. He shakes his head. No, no. Clutching the knob of his cane, he pulls himself to his feet and makes a slow journey to the bedroom. From the back of the closet he pulls the dress from the tissue paper where it's been stored all these decades. He wants to see her in it one last time.

Later, when the nieces are gone, he'll buy his first cigarettes in thirty years, light one up, pour himself a bourbon, and put on some Duke Ellington. He'll watch the smoke curl across the room and remember the feel of her in his arms.

Third Place Flash Fiction

From Week One Contest

The Ritual

Chinwe I. Ndubuka

"Oh," we gasped as we lost our vision.

Blackouts were so frequent, it should have been comical but no one laughed. We held our places—me, sitting cross-legged in front of the television; my brother, lying on his stomach holding a book; Aunty, on the settee with a plate of rice and plantain in her hands; Mother, next to her. The ceiling fan slowed to a stop and the African heat took over.

Outside the open window, overlaid with netting to keep mosquitoes out, two stars blinked. The settee creaked as Mother stood up. We used to navigate the furniture, bodies and staircase by memory, but now Mother used her cell phone's glow to guide her into the kitchen where the kerosene lamp sat at the end of the countertop, trimmed and filled. We heard her shake a matchbox and strike a match. Yellow light leaked into the living room, growing until she stood in the doorway casting shadows on the wall.

My brother found the flashlight and headed outside to the generator. After three pulls, it rumbled to life illuminating the room and sending the fan spinning. Just until bedtime. The lamp would last the night.

From Week One Contest—Prompt: smoking match image

Ephemeral

Frank Montagnino

Ephemeral, he thought, watching wisps of smoke waft from the matchstick. The perfect word. Perfect also to describe his relationship with Audra, although until yesterday he'd have chosen a different word – solid...or loving.

He remembered (hell, would never forget) the first time he'd seen her. She'd walked into his office, resumé at the ready. Truthfully, she had the job by the time she sat across from him, crossed those gorgeous legs and nailed him with her devastating green eyes.

As head of HR he had to show the new hire around, although it admittedly broke protocol to ask her to dinner that night. (She was new to town after all.) Then, at dinner it seemed so natural to offer to help her find a place to live in a safe neighborhood. She'd settled on a small cottage.

The relationship quickly escalated from friendly, to intimate, to all-consuming. Two days ago he'd picked up an engagement ring. Then yesterday, at the mall, he'd seen her kissing another man. A long, heartfelt kiss.

Ephemeral. That described their affair. He thought of another word as he flicked the dead match into the fire now engulfing the wall of the little cottage.

Bitch!

Burning for You

Karen Mocker Dabson

Like a tiny fairy's vapor trail, the smoke danced a mad fantasia against the blackness. Cradling her cheek, Sheila watched in fascination as the apparition curled from the match tip; but then the flames leapt up the bedroom curtains, eclipsing the sight and lighting the satisfaction in her eyes. She'd show him what a really hot night was like.

Déjà vu

Nancy Jo Allen

I see his face,
yet once more.
It's the same one
on the upholstery fabric
swatch. It was there in ghostly
image on the restaurant
window, a shadow
thrown from the pear tree
in the back garden,
and last night,
near the spinning blades
of the ceiling fan.
It's an ephemeral flash:
gone so quickly.
Now a spent match
swirls his image, too:
the prominent bridge
of his nose, flaring nostril,
deep socketed eyes
bushy brows. His left eye weeps.
It always weeps.
The hint of a cigarette
hangs below his nose.
Most disturbing is the scar
slicing his cheek
like the confluence
of the Missouri and Mississippi
rivers cut the Midwest.
I know not who he is,
nor why he makes himself
known to me in this déjà vu,
but he reveals himself
in unexpected ways, times, places.
I want to help him cross the veil.

Finalists Flash Fiction

From Week Two Contest—Prompt: image of porthole in the side of a wooden ship with crashing sea surround.

Leaving County Cork, 1837

Terry Allen

A young woman who appeared
to be sickly from the start died
after a fortnight and was buried
at sea with very little concern,
but the sight of it has born heavy
on my soul. She was sewn up
in a sheet with rocks at her feet.
Then all the Irish passengers
knelt down and prayed
for the poor dead woman
and when we were done,
she was thrown overboard
and slipped from our sight
below the waves,

and that was the end of her . . .

her death scarcely noticed
in a terrible storm.

"Oh God, take us out of poverty
and don't let us die with hunger,"
I heard myself say aloud
over and over and over again.

The Navy Way

Von Pittman

That December Sunday morning, sailors in lifeboats, launches, whaleboats, and other wooden craft dodged fire from Japanese fighter planes as they skittered around Pearl Harbor, retrieving sailors and marines from the mangled hulks on Battleship Row. Casualties delivered to shore collapsed on the beautifully trimmed Headquarters lawns. Some bled, some suffered burns; many died where they fell. The wooden craft made trip after trip, hauling in the casualties from the Arizona, the Oklahoma, the California, the many other capital ships. "We'll make the bastards pay!" became an immediate incantation. But all present knew their defeat was total, their revenge distant.

Admiral Husband E. Kimmel surveyed the sunken and twisted ships, the Rising Sun markings on the underside of the Japanese Imperial Navy's aircraft, the dead men in the harbor, the wooden boats trying to save those treading water. A spent bullet from a Japanese plane smacked into his dress white jacket, then fell to the ground. "It would have been kinder if it had killed me," he told his aide. There was no dissent. The entire fleet knew that after any defeat—or worse, humiliation—somebody had to "hang". Admiral Kimmel was a dead man walking.

From Week Three Contest—Prompt: image of an old typewriter in dark noir setting.

The Quick Brown Fox

Nancy Jo Allen

Her lips blow dust
from the the diary
in her hands;
pages open like a worn
umbrella rusted from rain
and full of holes.
Time retrogresses as she
descends wooden stairs
into her dusty basement
of memories jammed like keys
on a useless Olivetti
producing a cacophony
of letters that fail to express . . .

anything.

She learned to type
next to him in third period.
His eyes were kind.
That is what she remembers.
A sweet boy who
became a tumbling,
leaping cheerleader
for athletic events she
never attended.
His attempts to strike
her heart jammed—
missing contact
like that roller with no paper—
but the quick brown fox
jumped over the lazy dog,

so the lazy dog
never knew his kiss

Terry Allen

In long deep shadows
old keys strike ghostly pages —
pecking out lost lives.

* This is haiku, thus is untitled.

Finalists Flash Fiction

From Week Four Contest—Prompt: image of a man walking down a dirt road toward the setting sun.

Walking Toward the Edge of the World to See the Elephant

Terry Allen

He had thought that as long
as there were children
there would be circuses
and clowns but now
it was shutting down
after 146 years . . .

all gone . . .
the whitefaced clowns,
the fleshfaced tramps
all gone . . .

Now memories surround him
in soulful joy as he puts
one foot in front of the other.
So sad, but so happy.
He had been part
of the Greatest Show on Earth:

the clown cars,
sweet cotton candy,
midnight train whistles.
triple time bass bands,
old time calliopes,

and there were the crowds
and the dancing bears,
and all those balloons.

Now he hasn't put
his make-up on for months.

First, attendance dropped
and the elephants were retired
and then there were reports
of threatening clowns
popping up all around the country.

The New Orleans District
Attorney Jim Garrison
once said that someday there
would even be a book written
that blames JFK's assassination
on "retired circus clowns."

You know when a clown retires?
He thinks as he walks further
on toward the edge of the world.
It's when he dies . . .

or when he's shot
with a water canon
and does a double flip
backwards and a daisy
pops up out of his chest!

Solomon Gomes Roams

Frank Montagnino

One day, Solomon Gomes knocked on our door and asked if he could do some work in exchange for a meal and a place to stay the night.

Mother was taken by his polite manner; "yes ma'am," "let me fetch that for you ma'am." Besides, there was plenty of work to be done.

What started out to be a one or two-day stay became two of the happiest years our family ever had. Solomon was wise and funny and the place looked better immediately as he mowed, trimmed, painted and patched. He slept in the barn but took his meals with us, and his stories and his warmth turned our somber mealtimes into happy gatherings. We adored him, which is why we all cried when he told Mother that the time had come for him to be moving along.

I will never forget the sight of that beloved old man trudging down the muddy, rutted main road.

He was wearing the same work clothes as the day he appeared and he had his few meager belongings stuffed into his backpack – along with next month's rent money from the cookie jar and Grandma's good silver tea set.

A Double Escape

Kristian Wingo

All roads lead somewhere, thought James, smiling. The sun rose over the horizon but all he could see was farm.

He'd been kidnapped three days ago, plucked from a Chicago street as he was stumbling home late one night. He rode in their van, blindfolded, for hours. He had no idea where they'd taken him. The dirt road had no signs. He could be in Kansas, Canada, or just outside of Kankakee.

James's wife had paid the ransom quickly. Stacks of money stuffed into her son's backpack and driven to a remote spot all by herself. As the kidnappers expected, she was stupid. She followed orders exactly and didn't call the police. The money was untraceable.

James didn't think much of his wife either. For years, he'd wanted a way to escape marriage but keep his money. Now he had it.

Of course, the kidnappers had expected a different ending. Lying dead in an abandoned farmhouse, killed by their captive, was not part of the plan. For James, it was perfect. In taking him prisoner, they'd given him freedom.

James walked along the dirt road toward his new life wearing his stepson's backpack. A million dollars she can't touch.

Nonfiction

Nonfiction Judge

Jocelyn Cullity is the Director of the BFA in Creative Writing Program at Truman State University. She has published creative nonfiction and fiction. Her historical novel, *Amah & the Silk-Winged Pigeons*, was published last fall and is currently shortlisted for the 2017 Sarton Women's Book Award, the 2018 Eric Hoffer Montaigne Medal Award, and two 2017 Foreword INDIES Awards.

First Place Nonfiction

Twitch

Lori Younker

The professor of my Psychology class told us that suppressing our negative emotions and experiences was unhealthy and would lead to a state of repression. He described the two extreme tendencies. One denied reality while the other blew up outwardly. Tic. I remember thinking that I had no danger of becoming a suppressor. Rather, I was the other one, the one that enjoys the freedom of self-expression, the one that lets her feelings be known. Certainly, I was not a person who buried her feelings. Tic. I felt open and at peace with the world. Tic. I was comfortable with myself for the first time since I was ten years old. Tic.

The eye twitch says the opposite. Tic. Only, you can't see my eye as it spasms like a metronome on the piano. Tic. It's enough to drive me crazy. Tic. Someone, please smash that thing and let me be. Tic.

When my grandmother had her stroke, that would be my father's mother, tic, my job as English teacher was in full swing. Tic. Two new families from India, tic, one new family from Thailand, tic, and another family from the Philippines arrived in the second week of school. I needed to get them settled in their classrooms, tic, secure their immunizations, tic, teachers, and acclimate them to American life. Tic.

On her deathbed, my aunt handed my grandmother the phone. Her speech came out garbled. Tic. Yet, it had the music of the three words we love to hear. Tic. I wasn't there in her last days—and had I let myself—I would have cried for days. Tic.

The twitch began on my upper lip while talking to the school secretary. The annoying quiver on my upper lip should have been a signal of my deeper pain. Quiver, tic. I worked sixty hours a week and held down my Masters classes besides. Quiver, tic, tic.

The bottom lip quivered in sympathy. Top, top, quiver, quiver, tic.

At the funeral, tears ran down my face as I described my wondrous grandmother and her ways of grace, but as we left the sanctuary into the vestibule, we were greeted with hearty hugs and demands for socializing. There was no opportunity to cry. The twitches remained. Tic. Quiver. Tic.

Finally, the shower provided the place to let the tears flow. The privacy of hiding for an extra fifteen minutes in the bathroom went unnoticed by the family, and all the twitches ceased.

When my daughter Joanna was about fourteen years old, she announced her philosophy passionately, "I feel my feelings when I feel them. I don't hold them back. When I feel like crying, I cry."

Now, as a family physician, Joanna has surely learned to suppress her emotions. Responsibilities of adulthood, cultural norms—they all demand self-mastery. There are adult behaviors and childlike behaviors. Crying is for children.

Recently, my husband's father lay dying in hospice under this sister's loving care. We spent precious time at his bedside holding his hand, drying the tears from his eyes. I appreciated his gracious spirit, his words of thanks, of love, of blessing.

He passed on the 12th of December, just after we returned to Missouri. Tic. Someone suggested that we wait to have the memorial in early January. "Let's have Christmas and New Year's first." Tic.

At the memorial, my precious aunts and uncles sat two rows behind me in the funeral chapel. Sandwiched in the middle were my aging parents. Tic. I thought about all the goodbyes I have ahead of me in the near future. Tic. Hold it together, we have to get over to Marilyn's house to be available for setting up the food for the guests. Tic.

My five-year old grandson Jaben took my hand as we met in the aisle to walk out in front of all the guests. It was completely silent all around us. He asked a burning question, "What are we supposed to do next, Grama?"

I should have told him, "We cry." Tic.

I didn't cry when I was treated cruelly as a child by the crossing guard at the corner near Morrison Elementary School. Just let me get to school without being called Mustache Lady. Tic. By age seventeen, I was a seasoned repressor. Tic.

So tonight, I cry in the shower for all the times I should have owned my feelings, named them, and set them free.

I find that crying is particularly uncomfortable. I don't know if this one will be the big one of all cries. Each has its own internal clock. Tic. The release starts in the chest and moves to the shoulders. My body was built for this. It's okay. No ribs break. The cry will find its stopping point and leave me with an odd sense of stillness. For a moment there is . . . peace.

God said that in heaven He will wipe away every tear from our eyes. But for now? I will carry tissues.

These days **Lori Younker** explores the worlds of fiction and memoir. Two short story collections, *Mongolian Interior* and *Sioux Beside Me,* seek to capture her cross-cultural experiences. Many stories can be accessed at www. WorldSoBright.org.

Lori used her Master's degree in TESOL at the Graduate School of Missouri University (2010-2014) and currently as an instructor of ELLs in the public schools of Mexico, Missouri where she teaches children her first love: to read and write.

Second Place Nonfiction

Do You Want to do Lunch?

Lynn Strand McIntosh

Yesterday I volunteered as a lunch lady at an elementary school for their summer school session. This is a complicated job; you wear an apron supplied with extra straws, napkins and spoons. The children who need your assistance raise their hands and you aid them by opening plastic yogurts, milks, or the elusive string cheese. For this challenge the apron has scissors! I was fully armed and ready or the first barrage of students. I opened a milk, provided a straw, then opened a yogurt, provided a spoon, I got this. A darling little girl in a sparkly princess dress spilled her chocolate milk; I swooped in like Prince charming. My purple apron was becoming a cape, everyone is cute, everyone is polite and I am Super Lunchlady armed with blazing wet rags. The bell rings.

Second lunch and the students are a little older. Several students sit by themselves. Some perhaps by prearrangement for discipline issues, some for far deeper reasons, I observe and contemplate. Just then, a sweet girl takes a bite and cannot go any farther explaining with one hand in the air and one in her mouth, " I am going to lose my tooth, what do I do?" Fortunately, my co-lunch crusader is a medical professional, I beckon her and walk away. Then a young boy in a group raises his hand and I am quick to attend him and answer his query. He looks up at me concerned. "You know, I think I am the only Canadian here." An awkward silence surrounds us. Having nothing in my caped arsenal for this, he can see that I am perplexed. So he repeats, "No seriously, I think I am the only Canadian." I am desperate, I feel around in the apron; no customs forms, no French Dictionary, no flag with a big leaf on it . . . I am lost. I reply with a weak, "Could be?" I walk away slowly, shaking my head wondering if I let him down. Ahead I see a larger, curvy girl with her pants slipping off her backside. Will someone make fun of her? Can I just tell her or will that make a bigger scene? If someone teases her will she become anorexic in two years? Or could her parents sue me in turn for interfering? Beaten, I return to my corner.

My cape is now a wrinkled apron filled with lowly tools and I am reduced to straw giver and table wiper. The two boys in front of me are boasting and fake slugging it out, " I wouldn't let my bro go down like that, and I am not going down like that, soooo Kapow!" I am thinking that maybe someday maybe he can take over saving the earth with his false bravado. But will he have the tools? What if he runs into a lone toothless Canadian with saggy pants and body image issues? Suddenly, I am a tired old lady who fears for our future.

Lynn McIntosh is well into her sixties, lost some of her mind and none of her weight raising five sons in Columbia, Missouri. She remains in Columbia writing about somethings and nothings that come to her mind, before it is all gone. She would like to tell her friends and extended family what she thinks, but they have regrettably stopped asking. So she writes it down.

Nothing Was Normal About the Third Grade

Cortney Daniels

Nothing was normal about third grade. First of all, it wasn't a real third grade. It was a split room—half the kids there were in the second grade. And then there was Sister Mary Donald of the order of the Sisters of Mercy. You couldn't get a full impression of her because she was covered head-to-toe in her habit. Still it was wrong to think she was like all the other nuns bobbing down the halls in their habits. Sister Donald had the sweetest face, round and blue-eyed with a sparkly smile, but there was a formidable person under all that cloth that we could hardly defend ourselves against. You can't practice defense against something shapeless. I suspected she might be a bit lumpy, or maybe strapping, as she was fairly tall, and I had been reading Chad of the Circle C Ranch and imagined a world full of strapping women, like Chad's mom, wielding an axe over a desperate chicken's neck, somewhere in an unknown world, like the Sisters of Mercy, when all I had ever known was my suburbia where women were stay-at-home moms with babes and bottles held in exposed arms.

Third grade was the year I really got into trouble. First and second grades were just warm-ups. I don't even remember what I did, but Sister Mary Donald made me cry three times that year, and each time, after she'd honed in for the kill, she would feel a moment of tenderness and send me to the teachers' lounge across the hall where I got to cry just in front of the other teachers, and while doing so, breathe in the smoke that filled the room. I don't remember getting in trouble at home for these offenses, so my guess is she didn't tell.

She was also horrible to other kids, too, like Jim Brown. She taught Jim's brother Michael the year before in the first grade, but now the both of them were in our room—Michael in second and Jim in third. She would always wonder aloud why Jim couldn't be a better student, like Michael. Just after Christmas, the boys were absent for a few days, and it turned out that Jim had poked Michael in the eye with the bayonetted arm of one of those little green plastic soldiers all the kids played with then. Michael had to have surgery to put it back together and wore an eye-patch for about three months afterward. I'm sure now that it wasn't revenge, but at the time, I wasn't. The rest of us got a more mild measure of retribution against Sister Donald when Jerry Gust, who was in second grade, and his twin, Larry, would switch classrooms from time-to-time and she never figured it out.

But there were good things about third grade, too, which kept me from playing hooky and entering into a life of crime. For one thing, we had singing, and it was right in the classroom. Sister Mary Donald was very fond of music. In the beginning of the year, before she really knew our names, she took out her little round black pitch pipe, blew out a note, and had us sing it. Then she walked down all the rows of desks and called out about eight of us and informed us that we would be the altos. Ever since this very unprofessional method of selecting our place in the choir, I have been an alto. We practiced many songs and gave little concerts to the rest of the lower grades in our classroom over the year. I remember singing the bird songs: "Yellow Bird, up high in banana tree," and "Red, Red Robin." The others I've long forgotten. And we also got to not only pledge to the flag and the cross, but to sing different patriot songs at least once a day.

Another potentially good thing about the third grade was that we had a TV in our classroom. It sat on platform atop a rolling cart in the back corner of the room next to the coat closet. We never had a TV in my other classrooms, and I don't know what other classes had them, but I suspected most of them were somewhere in the 7th or 8th grades, so I felt like it was a gift. The purpose of the TV was, of course, to watch educational programs, and Chicago had Channel 11, which was public TV and full of education. We got all excited one morning when Sister Mary Donald told us that right after lunch, that very day, we would be taking a science lesson from TV. We had an hour for lunch, and as our school had no cafeteria and only a lunch room for kids who rode the bus and brought a sack lunch, I ran the four blocks home just so I wouldn't even be close to late getting back— the bell rang at 12:45 and I would not be tardy. Then I found out that all that running had been unnecessary, since my mother would be driving me back to school that afternoon. About once a month on a Friday, my mother volunteered in the office. She typed and looked very important. Afterward she would wait for me, and then the two of us would drive to pick up my brother from military school, where he spent the week and came home on the weekends. That afternoon, we were all excited about our science lesson, so after praying and pledging, Sister Donald turned on the TV for the first time all year. It turned out that the TV got all the normal channels that we got at home. As we waited patiently for Science on Channel 11 while she turned the dial, there was Walter Cronkite looking at us at 1:00 p.m. instead of 5:00 p.m.

That's when it all began--with Walter Cronkite telling us that President Kennedy had been shot. Sister Mary Donald quietly took out a pen and a slip of paper, wrote a note, took one of us aside, whispered into that ear while putting the note in that hand. The runner swooshed out of the room and headed for the office, and once the door had closed, an unknown noiselessness had overcome us—the fidgeting and hum of a classroom of 50 kids had vanished like steam does. The TV was on, and we were seeing live reports from Dallas, and no one even thought to ask about changing the channel to science. Very shortly, Walter Cronkite was back with us to say that the President was dead. Sister Mary Donald never changed the channel, and she never turned off the TV. Our principal, Sister Honora, came over the intercom not too long after we'd heard Walter Cronkite, and told the whole school what we already knew—that President Kennedy was dead.

We stayed in school that Friday afternoon, and our class got to watch TV and listen and work with our crayons. When the bell finally rang, I hurried downstairs to the office to meet up with my mother. I could tell that what happened to the President had shaken her, her certitude of manner replaced with something unknown: she handed me the key to our house, told me to walk home, go inside and stay there, and that it was fine to watch TV while she went to pick up my brother. First of all, I never ever had a house key. My best friend, Janet, who was in my grade at the public school, had one, and she wore it around her neck like a little golden cross. My mother, on the other hand, still locked me out of the house when she went on her errands. Second of all, every other school day, I was ordered to change out of my uniform and go outside—rain, shine, cold, or snow. But not today. Although TV annoyed her, and we weren't allowed to watch it during the week at all, it so happened that Nov. 22, 1963, was a Friday, so it's something I might have done. But by her behavior, I thought I might need to give her a report when she got home. That didn't happen, but it was the only time I was ever told to watch, except when President Kennedy was inaugurated, and then my mother and I watched together, and pledged allegiance to the flag. I guess that was because I was in kindergarten at the time, and not in school during the inauguration. I don't think my mother even voted for Kennedy. All I knew was that she was a poll worker and a Republican and a Nixon supporter. But she was also a Catholic, and ballots are secret.

That weekend, all of us watched a lot of TV. I didn't watch day and night, because, as my mother had trained me, I had the need to get outside and play and see my friends. But wherever I went in the neighborhood, even they were tuning in. By default, I saw Oswald get shot because I was at my friend, Janet's, and they were wrapped around their TV, like a necklace, she and her siblings—so I was, too. It was shocking for a third grader, but it seemed unreal and unknowable. Nobody really talked about it. The funeral was on Monday, so I guess we had the day off. And I remember watching that long weekend as the dead President lay in state while all the people wept in passing, and the funeral parade as the caissons rolled by, and the black dress and veil Mrs. Kennedy wore as she and the President's brothers walked behind, and the 21-gun salute.

Everything was different afterward, but I can't tell you how. It was subtle. Sister Mary Donald appeared unchanged, but how would that be possible— and we kept singing. But I remember being glad later in the spring when we had a school assembly and some of the teachers showed up with Beatle wigs on. I don't remember what the assembly was for, but the Beatles were helping to improve the mood around the country. God knows, we needed it right then, before race riots and civil disobedience and the Vietnam War and the next wave of assassinations. One warm and sunny May afternoon, just after school let out, I found a $20 bill on the grass right in front of church, and I was feeling like God gave me a gift. I never told anyone about it, not my mom, not my dad, especially not Sister Mary Donald. I felt lucky. And that about sums it up—nothing was normal about the third grade.

Cortney Daniels received her undergraduate and Masters' degrees from University of Missouri and is a graduate of the Iowa Writers' Workshop with an MFA in Poetry. Currently, she is working on a book of creative nonfiction. She has three grown children and a grandchild who all live elsewhere. She lives in Columbia, Missouri, with her spouse and cats, and works at a local nonprofit organization.

Can't We Just Be Friends?

Millicent Henry

I came to the kitchen this morning with my laptop to write an essay about women's issues. Instead, I've been sitting at the harvest table watching dozens of squirrels bury their nuts and wondering . . . wondering about their relationship status. Are they cousins, moms and pops with their pups or just friends? Since women do make up more than 50 percent of the population of these United States, I assume there are more gals than guys scampering around my back yard. After all, why would the rodent world be any different from ours?

Maybe I should write an essay about female squirrels. The scurry that inhabits the trees in our neighborhood is a mixed bag of colors—red, gray, brown, and black. Some are slow with age and lameness or disfigured by chopped tails; others seem more adept at nut gathering than many of their cohorts. Surely this species doesn't worry about politics, spirituality or socioeconomic place. (Who has more acorns?) I doubt they let these differences divide them like we females of the human kind do.

I marvel at the myriad of challenges that confront women in today's society: the young mother/professional coping with a stinky diaper while on a conference call: the recovering alcoholic living at the edge of poverty: the octogenarian fending off gentlemen with dementia at the care facility and women in the armed services protecting our freedoms at home and overseas. But as diverse as we are, I've come to believe that there is one, universal issue all women struggle with daily. I can almost hear a chorus of female voices asking, "What? What can that possibly be?"

Simply put, MEN—the other 49.2 percent of the populace, our male counterparts. Just for one day, keep track of every encounter you have with a member of the opposite sex. Amazing. I find that many of these interactions leave me feeling like we could do better—that men and women need to learn how to treat each other as you would a good friend—with respect, equality and fairness. Why is a friend-friend relationship between the sexes so hard to grow?

Perhaps the culture we live in makes platonic friendships between men and women almost impossible. There are firecracker-hot buttons of gender bias that keep males and females on opposite sides in an uneasy truce. Violence against women and sexual harassment continue. The wage gap between the sexes lessens but is not equal. Underrepresentation of women in political life and discrimination in academia improve at a snail's pace. These are serious matters and will only improve when both men and women decide to start a new conversation of change and mutual acceptance.

I've been married to the same man for forty-six years. In addition to my beautiful daughter, daughters-in-law, and granddaughters, I've been blessed with three sons, a son-in-law and three grandsons. I love them with all of my being. Now please don't think that I am some crazy misandrist, but I don't understand how males think, their quirky sense of humor or why they do such mysterious things. I'm still trying to figure out my husband's obsession with the minutiae of sports or why he cried at a KC Royals' World Series game, but not his grandma's funeral.

My first and last male friend was Steven. He was eight and I was seven when we met. We roamed the neighborhood like wild banshees, told each other our secret dreams and darkest fears. He stood up to the bullies who made fun of my buckteeth and comforted me when my father died the year I turned twelve. I was sure we'd be pals for life. Our wonderful closeness lasted until high school when he spoiled everything and asked me out on a date. I turned him down and our friendship died a slow and painful death.

"That's precisely the reason why men and women can't sustain platonic friendships," writes author, Donna Flagg, in Psychology Today. "Between cross-gender friends, sexual tension often seethes beneath the surface until one or both people give in to the attraction." What I find most interesting is her last explanation for the failure of these friendships. Flagg says, "The trouble really has nothing to do with the two friends at all. Rather, it's a jealous girlfriend, boyfriend or spouse who forbids it. So when women and men 'can't' be friends, it's usually because someone who claims to love you says, 'You're not allowed.'"

"Dang," I say to myself. "That's not right."

While I've been daydreaming, the screen on my laptop has faded to black and there are no words on the page. Frustrated, I give up on the essay today, and succumb to the yeasty aroma of homemade potato bread, cooling on the counter. I cut a thick slice, smear it with persimmon butter, and give silent thanks to the squirrels for saving me some fruit. Flame-red leaves plummet earthward from a towering maple leaving behind a dark silhouette against the icy sky. Thirty feet high, an irregular blob of sticks and leaves nestles in the curve of the tree trunk. Who lives there, I wonder—Great Grandma, The Flying Rodent Rock Band or just two cross-squirrel friends?

My thoughts swirl back to the time I allowed insecurities and fear to rule my life. On December 21st, winter solstice dawned gray and heavy, the air filled with the promise of snow. I was struggling to find myself. At the age

Nonfiction

of forty, I was the new mother of a beautiful baby boy, born sixteen years after my first son. Holiday preparations were frantic and haphazard. And that morning, the stack of Christmas cards that avalanched off the desk to land at my feet made me cry. How would I ever answer them all?

Sitting gingerly on the floor, I stacked the cards into piles. When I picked up the last one, my fingers froze on the envelope. The letter was addressed to me in bold and familiar handwriting. In the upper corner was the name of my long-ago sweetheart from college. I panicked. Why would he contact me after 20 years? Would my husband be upset? Why did my heart beat a little faster? Should I even open it?

Temptation won. I took the letter to my office, shut the door and ripped through the paper. Inside was a traditional Christmas card. But it was the hand-written note on the inside that shook me. He inquired about my family and wished us a Happy Holiday. His last line was, "I'd very much like to hear from you." And then he listed his phone number and address.

I chose not to respond to my former boyfriend's gentle request, using the excuse that my husband might be jealous. In truth, I never told him about the letter until years later. The following February, my college alumni magazine arrived. On page five was the stunning announcement of his death. He had been dying of Multiple Myeloma as he wrote that Christmas card.

I'm haunted by a deep sense of shame and disappointment that I was not strong enough to be his friend when he reached out to me; I denied both of us the opportunity to acknowledge the worth of our past relationship and to say our good-byes—a lesson learned too late.

School is out. Frightened squirrels take flight up the shagbark hickory in a parade of fluffy tails as ten middle schoolers straggle across the footbridge at the back of our property. The boys lead the way—no coats on—throwing sticks and rocks into the quiescent stream. Twenty yards behind follow the girls chattering nonstop. The impulse to rush out onto the deck is almost overpowering. I want to yell at them, "Walk with each other. Talk to each other, please. It's okay to be friends."

Instead, I rail at the centuries-old mores that linger in our culture. The days when women stayed at home and men went to work no longer exist. Now males and females play, work and coexist in the same arenas, becoming more androgynous as societal roles change. Just for fun, try to imagine how different the world might be if Anthony and Cleopatra were friends instead of lovers or Harry and Sally had stayed mixed-gender buddies. Michael Monsour, a professor of communications at UCDenver believes, "The movie, *When Harry Met Sally*, set the potential for male-female friendships back about twenty-five years."

Earlier this week, twelve women from my church met for breakfast at a local restaurant. We savored the creamy hollandaise of eggs Benedict and the comfort of shade-grown coffee. An easy conversation flowed until I asked the group, "Have you ever or do you now have a close male friend?"

Oh. My. Gosh. For over an hour, my question sparked an intense dialogue. Each woman there wanted and needed to tell her story. Given our disparate ages, thirties to eighty-ish, we represented three generations. Many spoke of their own closed mindedness toward establishing a nonsexual relationship with men. A few admitted that they, themselves, were jealous wives or had controlling husbands. Another woman told of being falsely accused of having an affair when seen talking and laughing with a man who was not her husband at a party. Only one came forward and confessed that she enjoyed several male friendships where sex was not an issue.

When I arrived home, I asked my son, who was painting his cabinet doors in our basement, if he had any close female friends? He thought for long minutes before he answered. "I used to before I got married. But now I only spend time with other women besides my wife in a group setting." I rest my case. What must happen to stop this "voluntary gender segregation?"

There is good news. My son-in-law, a psychologist and outreach counselor at a large high school, states that the climate among today's teenagers and young adults is evolving. "More and more," he says, "I see a boy and girl hanging out together not as boyfriend and girlfriend but just as pals." He goes on to point out that this change in behavior has created a more positive and healthy environment in the school setting.

As I look to the future with resolve, I am thankful to be part of several small writing groups. I'm excited that a number of gentlemen are committed members. Their experiences, their perspectives, and their unconditional friendships have enriched my life and broadened my thoughts immeasurably. My husband, a cribbage enthusiast, often plays with another woman down the street. Almost every day my neighbor, a former professional football player, greets me with a bear hug and a detailed update on the local sport's scene. We are learning how to be friends.

As we talk, a shower of acorns rains down upon us.

Magic Makeup

Billie Holladay Skelley

Any outing with my four, young children required planning, organization, and patience. It always seemed that getting everyone ready and in the car by a certain time was like moving an entire army—even when we were just venturing out for a couple of errands. Despite my best efforts at being an orderly and efficient leader of this troop, these excursions were often hectic, chaotic, and traumatic. Occasionally, they were even funny.

Before being cleared for any away mission, we had to have diapers, extra underwear, wipes, exchanges of clothes, and a two-seat stroller in the transport vehicle. Certain foods, drinks, and cups were also necessary. If these nutritional items were not present, the car could be forced to stop at the closest eating establishment to procure essential nourishment for the suddenly starving and screaming inhabitants. I accepted that clothing and food were necessary for any successful maneuver, but we also had to pack "the yellow blanket," a stuffed Eeyore, a gorilla named "Digit," a NASA rocket, a Batman cape, two "My Little Ponies" and their combs, a Strawberry Shortcake purse, and an odd assortment of books and other items.

I often wondered why we just couldn't get up and leave. I also wondered why my children considered these "things" absolutely vital for a trip. Experience had taught me, however, these items were critical. If there was to be any chance of us completing a mission successfully, these "things" had to be found, placed in the vehicle, and be located within a certain hand's reach.

As quartermaster of this army, I tried to collect all necessary items in one area before we even attempted to depart. I also checked the car, car seats, and seat belts for readiness. No matter how I prepared, however, the capture, restraint, and confinement of four children, while trying to position critical supplies, proved to be loud and chaotic. Consequently, our departures were almost always stressful.

During these withdrawal operations, there was no opportunity or time for me to work on my personal appearance. I often realized, as the car exited the garage, that I did not look very presentable. It was too dangerous, however, to stop the car, to go back inside, and to try to make improvements. Once these troops returned to base, there was little chance they could be moved again. It was best to just keep advancing forward. As a result, I often appeared in public looking somewhere between a disheveled sea urchin and a dark-eyed Medusa.

On one of these trips, while trying to purchase more diapers and wipes, I happened to see myself in a store window. I realized, rather than Medusa, I looked more like a spotted leopard wearing a lion's mane. I decided I had reached a new low, even for me. The least I could do, I thought, was to comb my hair and put on a little makeup to hide some of my stressful blemishes—especially on my forehead. I vowed, before our next venture into the public domain, I would improve my appearance.

Consequently, prior to our next outing, I quickly sat down in front of the mirror beside my bed. The blemishes on my forehead made me look like I either had hives, herpes, or chicken pox. I couldn't decide which. For a brief moment, I considered that I might have contracted some exotic disease, but since I had not been anywhere exotic in years, I concluded it must just be me.

Using a small tube of concealer, I tried to cover my contagious-looking marks. As I dabbed my forehead, I noticed my six-year-old son was staring intently at me. Not comfortable being scrutinized so closely, I asked him if everything was okay. He nodded, affirming that all was good, but his eyes were still attentively focused on my forehead.

Finally, he said, "What are you doing?"

"I'm just putting on a little makeup so we can go do our errands," I answered.

I continued to dab at the lesions on my forehead.

"I never saw you do that before."

"Well," I answered truthfully, "I need to do it today, and I need to start doing it every day."

"Okay," he answered. "But how does it work?"

"I just put it on," I answered.

Thinking the issue was resolved, I finished and put the cap on the concealer. Looking at myself in the mirror, I decided I was like the soldier who paints his face to camouflage it so that he blends in with the surrounding vegetation or terrain. I was now painted and ready for whatever maneuver or battle came my way.

I loaded up the car, and we went to the grocery store, pharmacy, post office, barber shop, and dry cleaners. At each stop, we all got out of the car, taking whatever supplies were deemed essential for that particular excursion. When that task was accomplished, we all got back in the car for the next challenge. Five hours later, and after several repetitions of "out of the car" and "back in the car," we completed our errands and returned home.

When my husband came home that evening, he asked my son how the day had gone.

"Fine," my six-year-old answered.

"What did you do?" asked my husband.

"We went grocery shopping, mailed stuff, got haircuts, and picked up dry-cleaned clothes."

Knowing that such a multipronged attack could be difficult with two young children, a toddler, and a baby, my husband repeated, "So everything went okay?"

"Yes," my son answered. "Mommy got this new medicine that she puts on her forehead. It helps her make up her mind where we are going and what we're doing. So, everything went fine."

Confused, my husband immediately inquired about my "magic" medicine. It took a few minutes for us to figure out what my son was talking about. When we finally understood that our son thought I was putting makeup on my forehead to help me "make up" my mind, my husband and I laughed for at least fifteen minutes.

I always thought I was pretty good at explaining things to my children, but I was amazed how my son could interpret my simple act of putting on makeup so differently. I had to admit, however, from his point of view, his assumption was perfectly logical. Even after we explained the real purpose of makeup to him, my son would still say, every time he saw me putting it on, "Mommy is trying to make up her mind what to do!"

It became a family joke—with me at the center of the laughter.

In time, the joke grew as my little tube of concealer expanded into a full cosmetic bag containing lipstick, foundation, rouge, eye shadow, mascara, and lotion. As time went on and my stress levels increased, I realized I needed more and more products to try to look presentable. Based on old photographs of myself that keep turning up, my camouflage attempts were never very successful. In these pictures, I usually look like a rosy-cheeked Medusa or a leopard with lipstick. (These old photographs have been known to become casualties of the fire in the fireplace! I feel some historical documents do not need to be preserved!)

Thirty years have passed since that original makeup incident, but every time, in the intervening years, when I have put on any makeup, I always remember what my son thought I was doing, and I have to smile. It reminds me how often a parent can see one thing and a child can see something entirely different. My makeup may not have helped me to make up my mind, but after that experience, it did make me pause more often as a parent and try to consider things more from my children's point of view.

I continue to believe we needed an excessive number of items loaded in the car for a victorious outing, but I came to accept, from my children's point of view, that their items were as essential to them as my duffel bag of makeup became to me.

Night Noises in Krakow

Suzanne Connelly Pautler

Faces, along with strange images, zoomed close, then far, while the English accented female voice repeated, "you are over the speed limit, you are over the speed limit." I sat up, ripped off my eye mask, and pushed the covers off my sweating body. It was 2:40 a.m.

What's going on? I thought, irritated that I was in this anxious state. It was the first time my sleep was so agitated in the week and a half of sleeping in a variety of lodgings in Eastern Europe.

Then I heard it. Outside our apartment door, loud noises reverberated from the marble stairwell inside this pre-World War II, five-story building in Krakow, Poland. At first it sounded like someone hitting or kicking a door somewhere in the three stories below. I crept to our apartment door and listened. Another loud bang and the door rattled from forceful pressure below. I stepped back.

From the stairwell, footsteps and clanging echoed, like someone hitting against the metal hand rails. It wasn't constant, like maybe the person paused or possibly was trying to be quiet, but couldn't. I listened and hoped the person was drunk and having trouble finding his apartment. After more clinks, clanks, and the sound of footsteps on the stairs, I heard a deep voice close enough that I knew it was a man. The heels of his shoes clicked on the stairs as he came up and closer to our level in the building.

I turned the lights out in our apartment, so it was dark under our door.

Quietly, I went to my sleeping husband and whispered in his ear. Through the hum of his CPAP machine, he seemed to sort of hear me, but stayed asleep. I decided it was more important for me to listen for the noises outside our door, than to startle him awake, possibly causing him to call out loudly. He could sleep for now.

I hoped the man in the stairwell wouldn't knock anyone's door in. I held my cell phone close and wondered what I'd do if he forced our door. The tall coat tree could be a weapon, but it didn't seem very sturdy. I decided I'd turn the phone flashlight on, shine it in his eyes, and scream. I backed away the few feet to the doorway of our bedroom, phone ready.

His steps grew louder. It seemed he went past our door and higher. There were light footsteps on the floor of the apartment above me, at the top of the building. I knew others had to have been awakened by all the noise.

His steps retreated down and past our door. A dog yapped from an apartment below. He quickly came back up and tried our door knob. The dog barked again. I was shaking.

I googled on my phone to confirm that the emergency number for Europe is "112". I hoped someone else, someone who spoke Polish, had called the police.

Paper rustled outside our door. I froze. He was only about six feet from me. The old apartment door was all that separated us. "Playhouse Apartment" is written on a sign outside our door. Maybe it attracted him, the only door in the building with a sign. Finally, footsteps clicked down the stairs.

I quietly found the printout with the apartment address and dialed "112". A lady answered, and I whispered, "English. I'm in Krakow, Poland. Someone is in the stairwell and tried our doorknob. I'm scared." Suddenly a recording started playing on the phone.

The dog below barked frantically. Loud footsteps came up again. Our door handle was noisily turned and jiggled.

I ended the call and my phone immediately vibrated. A local dispatcher had called me back. I crept to the kitchen, where I hopefully wouldn't be heard. My mouth was very dry as I turned on my phone flashlight, put on my reading glasses, and quietly read the apartment address one letter at a time to the emergency person. The paper shook in my trembling hand. He had trouble understanding me. Oh, I thought, surely a local person had called. I finally relayed enough of the address that he finished it.

Then he asked the building number. Addresses are different here. I studied it and realized the building is "6". I told him surely someone else had called. He then realized where I was and said there had been other calls from the building and the police were on their way. We hung up.

I moved to the window, stood still, listened, and waited. The dog barked off and on as the rattling continued in the stairwell.

Finally, emergency lights flashed blue, far below in the street. After more minutes, there were male voices in the stairwell. Just talking, not loud. Steps retreated.

I videoed from the front window, down the four levels to the police van, and narrated what had just happened. I think I needed someone to talk to, even if it was me.

The side door of the police van slid open. I couldn't see who got in. More minutes passed, then an officer went to the driver's door. The police van slowly drove away. Blue lights flashed across the nearby buildings.

Light footsteps creaked above. The sounds of doors clicking open echoed from the stairwell. People quietly talked, no doubt sharing what had happened and how they felt. The yapping dog barked loudly, most likely outside his apartment with his owner. I decided not to open my door. I can't speak their language, so it wouldn't do any good.

I'm still listening as I write this. I hope there really was just one person. There are still noises in the building. I smell cigarette smoke. Our door handle is gently wiggling. The owners of the apartment must be checking on us. I'm glad the old wooden door has two locks, but wonder if the screws and wood would keep an intruder out. Luckily this person didn't forcefully try to kick the door in.

My husband is still asleep. I'm not sure he'll believe what happened.

Now, how do I settle down and try to sleep?

Red, White, and Blue Babies

Billie Holladay Skelley

Six-month-old Baby María is crying. Her skin has a blue tinge, and her lips are almost navy. She is a new admission to our surgical floor, but Baby María is not new to the hospital. A cardiac catheterization and echocardiogram have confirmed she has tetralogy of Fallot—a condition involving four related heart defects.

Baby María has a hole between the lower chambers of her heart, and her main blood vessel, the aorta, is in the wrong place. It lies over both lower chambers instead of just the left chamber. In addition, she has a narrowing or obstruction from her heart to her lungs, and the muscle surrounding her lower right heart chamber is greatly thickened. She appears to be a "blue baby" because oxygen-poor blood is being pumped through her body. It is traveling through the hole in the wall between the right and left chambers instead of being pumped to the lungs.

Baby María's parents appear worried and distressed. Their apprehension is understandable. Their child has had this condition since birth, and their last six months have been filled with fear and foreboding. Now their daughter is being admitted for open heart surgery to repair the four defects, and their anxiety, nervousness, and concern is evident. They know their child has a serious problem, and they recognize the surgical repair is complicated. The tension in the room is palpable.

As the admitting nurse, I sit down with the family to discuss what they can expect during their hospital stay. As I start, their questions begin to flow like water breaching a dam. What are Baby María's chances? Could she die on the operating table? How long will she be in surgery? Will the surgery be curative? Who will do the actual surgery? Who will be the anesthesiologist? Will their pediatric cardiologist be there? Who will take care of her afterwards?

I try to answer their questions and calm their fears. I explain that the cardiovascular surgeon in charge of Baby María's care is from India, and he has performed many tetralogy of Fallot repairs. He will likely be assisted by a surgeon from the Philippines, as well as an assistant from Alabama. I explain that they will soon meet the pediatric anesthesiologist assigned to Baby María's case, and I believe she is from Lebanon. Many nurses, pharmacists, and therapists from many different backgrounds and locations will be involved in their child's care.

As I attempt to answer these questions, it occurs to me that Baby María's medical team reflects what is best about America. The team is a group of very different people working together for a common goal. We are all united in using our energies and talents to achieve the best care possible for our patient, and we realize no one can do it alone. Each person is essential for success. It takes the team working together as partners to make everything work. Team members are appreciated for what they do, their skills, and what they bring to the team. No one cares what your country of origin is, the color of your skin, or which religion you follow. We are better because of our varied training programs, our different educational pursuits, and our divergent healthcare experiences. We are stronger because of our differences, but because we are all united in one effort, somehow our differences seem less significant.

It also occurs to me that maybe doctors and nurses have an advantage over other people. Experience has taught us that when people are truly ill, many of the perceived, overt differences, which people often focus on, vanish. Most sick patients, for example, appreciate assistance from any hand. It doesn't matter the color of the hand or its background. If you truly have a high fever, you appreciate a cool cloth from anyone—someone like you or someone very different. If you are extremely thirsty, you will delight in a cool glass of water no matter who brings it to you. Suffering is universal, and I have seen firsthand that when patients truly experience pain, they are extremely grateful to whomever provides relief—regardless of their nationality, language, or expertise.

Besides, a medical team does not have time to dwell on differences. There are so many people in need, the focus has to be on providing care. Moreover, I think, on a biological level, healthcare professionals realize that all people are pretty much the same. We all have lungs, kidneys, stomachs, and brains that can go awry and cause problems. We all have bones that can break, limit mobility, and cause pain. We all grow old and have similar medical problems associated with aging. Above all, on an operating table with organs exposed, we look pretty much the same. We all bleed red blood. Maybe healthcare providers just see patients as people. Maybe we are more inclusive because we see, from a medical point of view, that people do belong to one race—the human race.

It takes a few days in intensive care and a few more on the surgical floor, but Baby María's surgery and hospitalization go well. I see her again to prepare her parents for her discharge from the hospital. With oxygen-rich blood now circulating through her body, she is no longer a "blue baby." She has a rosy glow, and her red lips are curved in a smile. Best of all, she now has hope for an active and happy life. Her parents are greatly relieved and looking forward to taking their only child home. I tell them that being a part of the diverse team that worked together to transform their child from an ill "blue baby" to a healthy rosy-red child was a privilege—and I mean it—because being part of Baby María's medical team reminded me why I believe America is so wonderful.

We may begin life as babies of various colors and backgrounds, but as Americans, we all represent the red, white, and blue. We may have tensions and worries, but careful observation always reveals that our similarities outnumber our differences. We may have fears and concerns, but by and large, we are united by the principles that define our country and the goals we have established as a nation. Just like our medical team, our country pools its various talents for the benefit of its people—and when we work together, we can solve even the most complicated problems. For me, this is what makes America a great nation, and it is why I am proud to be an American.

Sweet Soles

Sheree K. Nielsen

There's an unspoken truth about shoes left at the beach. No matter how long you leave them on the boardwalk or in the sand, chances are, when you return from your walk or swim or kite flying, they'll be there waiting for you . . . eager to caress and soothe your tired, exfoliated feet, guiding you back to your house by the sea, Schwinn bicycle, or Jeep.

Whether they're Teva black flip flops, leather Birkenstocks, or the strappy gold metallic kind, sandals gather together for a shoe fest of their own.

I wonder what they'd say to each other if they could talk?

"Slow down!" or "You need a pedicure" or "Your soles are killing me!" or even "You're so soft and smooth".

They say you can tell a lot about someone by their shoes. I suppose the same applies for sandals.

I know mine are the 'comfort' Teva's – the longer they're worn, they conform to my feet. The fabric straps once ebony black, have faded to a pleasant midnight-purple, bleached by the sun and kissed by my toes.

Sometimes they require a good 'old Dawn dish liquid washing after particles of sand get stuck in the cracks of my flip flops, or pick up smells from the beach.

Every time I slip on those flip flops, they remind me of all the places I've visited, and countless adventures I've yet to experience.

Over the years, I've purchased a couple more pair of sandals. But somehow, I end up choosing the seasoned black Teva's over all the others.

My husband says beach sandals remind me of the diversity in this world, and how each person, like sandals, can be different from one another. Some sandals have thick complex stitching or expensive leather. Others are as simple and humble as a molded ninety-nine cent pair of plastic flip flops from the Dollar Store.

Eyeing those sandals lined up along the boardwalk steps, or scattered in the sand, I realize people have chosen to trust each other. When we kick off our shoes, we leave worries behind, allowing the beach to invigorate, renew and strengthen our minds and bodies. We're left vulnerable – open to sights and sounds, and even conversations with perfect strangers.

And just like our naked soles at the beach, we become one with each other.

Travels in Syria: A True Story

Drew Coons

"I want your address. I will come to America. I will keel you." The large, surly Arab looked us in the eye as he spoke. As my wife and I glanced at each other, she whispered, "He's kidding, right?" After all, he could kill us right then and there if he really wanted to. Surely this must be a form of Arabic humor, we thought. Rather than risk provoking him by refusing and still remain on the safe side, we only gave him our office address.

We traveled through Syria just before the civil war there started. We spoke through a translator to large groups of Christians and some Muslims about having rewarding marriage relationships. We taught in all the places you've seen on the news: Aleppo, Homs, Damascus. About 5% of Syrians are considered Christian—that is, born of Christian parents. Local Christians organized our engagements.

"You are the head of the snake!" another Arab snarled at us regarding America. But not all Syrians felt that way. One young man who served as a tour guide for us expressed admiration for the US. Dressed in jeans and a polo shirt, he studiously acted American and used American lingo. This marked him in Syrian culture as a rebel, a bad boy. Why would he do this? We passed three pretty Muslim teenage girls completely covered by black hijabs except for their faces. Their expressive eyes had been highlighted with heavy false eyelashes and dark liner. To our surprise, the girls took the initiative to call out flirtatiously to the bad boy. He shrugged them off. "Happens all the time," he explained.

Despite a few detractors, most Syrians are hospitable and welcomed us warmly. We generally felt safe when under the protection of our hosts, especially when they housed us in a convent. Hospitality in Syria is equated to personal honor like depicted in the Bible's Old Testament. Many Syrians invited us into their homes where they went to tremendous effort to prepare special Arab dishes for us. One charming Arab custom is that a guest is supposed to adamantly deny food, even if he is starving. The host then insists and, if necessary, takes the guest's plate and piles it with food. Having been in several Arab cultures previously, we knew and followed the customs. This required us to eat and praise everything regardless of any potential consequences.

And consequences there were. After a week, I became as sick as any tourist to Mexico has ever been. Fortunately, we take anti-diarrhea and stomach medicines along on our trips so that we can do our job no matter how badly we feel. But the generous invitations to Arab homes continued to come. Remember the Arab custom about food and hospitality? Regardless of how much I insisted that I couldn't eat, our gracious hosts knew better. I can now testify from personal experience, "I can do all things through Christ who strengthens me."

Every culture also has surprises. Syrians are bird fanciers. Most have in their homes pampered pet birds—parrots, canaries, doves—which are extraordinarily tame and appear to enjoy family festivities. The biggest public activity on Saturdays in Damascus is the "pigeon exchange." Hundreds of men, young and old, gather all morning at an outdoor rendezvous buying, selling, and trading pet birds. Now whenever western media shows Arabs in angry mobs, I also remember the other picture: coarse-looking men gently handling and admiring pigeons.

Our speaking engagements required travel between towns. Buses are the most economical and convenient transport. We had to take one five-hour trip between Aleppo and Damascus without an Arabic-speaking guide. Our hosts bought our tickets and put us on the "luxury express" bus. We enjoyed riding through the barren Syrian desert in cool air-conditioned comfort. About halfway to our destination, the bus stopped in a smaller town. We had been told by our hosts before leaving Aleppo that a stopover of fifteen to twenty minutes would give us a break. I got off the bus to look around and use the toilet.

In my absence, police commandeered the luxury bus and moved it. I came back to find our comfortable bus and my wife had vanished. Nobody could understand my English as I asked where the bus and my wife had gone. Close to panic and watched by hundreds of robed Arabs, I ran everywhere, looking into every bus. Finally, through a thick hedge, I glimpsed a large vehicle moving. After climbing over a ten-foot wrought-iron fence and fighting through the hedge, I found a second bus terminal. There I discovered my wife making quite a spectacle of herself protecting our luggage and trying to keep an alternate bus to Damascus from pulling away and leaving us behind. Someone banged on the side of the bus. The driver stopped just long enough for us to jump on with our suitcases.

This local bus could only be described as decidedly non-luxury, and we had lost our nice seats. In Syria, a woman has the right to not sit next to any man who isn't her husband. Since two seats together no longer remained available, the driver invited my wife to sit in the front next to another woman who traveled alone. I ended up sitting shoulder-to-shoulder on the back bench of the bus with a ragged group of desert dwellers. Their swarthy un-shaven looks would have frightened the mujahedeen's "holy warriors," let alone me. All they needed was bandoleers of bullets across their chests to be picture perfect. Soon, the warm afternoon air and motion of the bus lulled one man next to me to sleep. His turbaned head gradually slipped over onto my shoulder. I "accidentally" kicked his leg, which startled him awake. But gradually his head nodded over onto me again. I sat there thinking, Not everybody gets a chance to do this. He woke from his nap as we pulled into Damascus and never seemed to notice his pillow.

Our talks on marriage and relationships in Syria were a sensation. The crowds laughed at our stories and responded with gratitude. Arabs clustered around us after every session expressing personal difficulties with relationships and asking sincere questions. Even the undercover police monitoring us seemed to enjoy our presentations. You can always pick secret police out of an audience because they don't bring a spouse and nobody sits next to them.

Serving our fellow man, especially those very different from ourselves, is truly a privilege and an adventure. Adventures are not necessarily fun at the time. And yet, if we embrace them, they will enrich our lives and our understanding of others.

When I Shot My Neighbor: A True Story

Drew Coons

Do you remember your biggest ever surprise? Mine came on a pre-dawn Christmas morning not long after my eighth birthday. Under the Christmas tree I found a brand new 20-gauge shotgun. You might be thinking, *That is a surprise.* Some may shudder at the thought of giving a real gun to an eight-year-old. My father, however, had a plan. As a gun enthusiast himself, he wanted to teach his oldest son responsibility.

That afternoon he took me into the country to try out my new shotgun. But no paper target or old can would suffice for us. Instead, Dad started flinging a round, flat target called a clay pigeon into the air. In flight, the clay pigeon looked like a thin, black line. The target flew away from us so fast that if I blinked, it was gone. At barely eight years old and small for my age, I could hardly hold the gun up. The best I could manage was trying to cover the clay pigeon with the muzzle of the gun and pulling the trigger. After each shot the shotgun's recoil hurt terribly, worse than any spanking. I didn't know much about shooting. I did know instinctively that a man wouldn't acknowledge any amount of recoil pain. And so neither did I.

Eventually I managed to clip a couple of the targets and even smashed one. Dad shouted out with pride in his son. Then my father gave me an unexpected instruction. "I want you to shoot that tree." And he indicated a little pine tree about the size of a baseball bat handle.

"Shoot the tree?" I asked.

"Yes, shoot the tree," he repeated.

Now this still target was more to my liking. No way that this pine tree could fly away. Carefully taking aim and firing, I hit the little pine squarely at my eye level. The damage to the tree shocked me. All the bark had been torn away and the strong wood riddled. "Now, what do you think would happen if you accidentally shot a man?" my father asked. No answer was necessary. I fully understood the gun safety lesson.

A couple of weeks later our whole family had gone on an outing in the country. My dad pointed into a little gully. "I'll bet there are some quail in there," he predicted. Then he pulled my shotgun out of the car trunk and handed it to me along with a couple of shotgun shells. My mother, little brother, and sister could watch me get my first birds. Dad pointed to the right. "I'll go around here. The birds will flush out that way," he explained, waving to the left. "You know what to do."

And I did know what to do. There I stood, an eight-year-old with his finger on the trigger of a loaded gun. With the others watching, I couldn't let those birds escape. My father started around the gully and the birds flew up, but not as he had expected. The birds flew directly between my father and me. Rather than fire, I calmly watched the quail fly away with the gun pointed safely skyward. The safety lesson of the pine tree had saved my father's life. As he came walking back, my mother felt understandably shaken. She screamed, "I thought you were dead! He could have shot you!"

"It's just a good thing he didn't," Dad answered with gruff pride in his son. That day I felt like a man for the very first time.

Nearly thirty years later, my wife and I lived at the edge of a subdivision with large overgrown fields behind us. On a beautiful crisp fall afternoon, I was enjoying a walk around the backyard. To my surprise a covey of wild quail flew over my head and spread out in the fields. I got my shotgun and went to find the hiding birds. The man who owned the fields was a friend from my church. His son, a young man of 22, heard me shooting at the quail. He brought his shotgun and joined me. As we walked and talked, some quail flew up back toward the subdivision. Without thinking, I fired at them. Immediately, I knew that I had made a mistake. Nobody will ever know, I thought.

We continued hunting a while longer, but saw no more birds. I invited him back to my house. To our surprise, my young friend's wife was waiting there in our kitchen with my wife. "You guys stay inside!" she pleaded. "Somebody in the neighborhood has been shot. The police are looking for who did it."

Looking out the front window, I saw a sheriff's patrol car cruising slowly down our street, trying to get a bearing on the shooting. Overcome by guilt, I threw open the front door and ran to catch the police car. Grabbing the door handle, I confessed, "It was me! I shot toward the houses!"

The patrol car stopped, the door opened, and a huge deputy emerged. He was an African American man big enough to wring my skinny neck on the spot. At that moment, a neck wringing would have come as a relief. But he stood there with his hands on his hips just looking at me. "Son, you are a grown man. You should know better than to be so careless. Now, you go tell that lady that you're sorry." And he pointed to the house of our best friends.

Apparently, a few of the shotgun pellets had struck our friend Sherri. Fortunately, those pellets had been spent and hadn't penetrated her skin. The deputy didn't have to force me. Being truly repentant, I approached her, confessed, and asked for forgiveness.

Nonfiction

When Sherri saw who had shot her, she said, "If it had been anybody but you, I would give them a piece of my mind." Then she proceeded to give me all of her mind. She was understandably more upset because her baby had also been outside and could just as easily have been hit. I deserved every bit of her ire. I stayed silently nodding as long as she had anything to say. Her tirade seemed to last forever, but probably was only twenty minutes. After releasing her emotions, Sherri did fully forgive me and sent me home. Our friendship was unaffected.

As I walked home in shame and relief, I realized, You did better handling a gun when you were an eight-year-old boy. To this day, I am extremely cautious using firearms and have taught many boys and girls to be the same.

Plus, I learned a deeper lesson. Sometimes we learn the right thing to do from a young age, but when we are grown, we seem to forget or get careless. Perhaps overconfidence is a danger that comes with being an adult. To truly be men, we frequently just need to remember to do what we know is right, and what our fathers taught us.

Zipping Through Vegas

Deb Sutton

I almost died on a Ferris Wheel.

Can you die from fear? It wasn't even fear for myself. At seven months pregnant, I was wedged in that thing pretty good, but I had no business being on a Ferris Wheel. My two-year-old son, Ryan, had begged me to take him. We were at Six Flags over Texas and the point was to ride the rides. It would be fun.

Except it wasn't.

My first indication of trouble came when we pulled the bar down to hold us in. It didn't go down all the way because of my huge baby belly, and I realized Ryan could slip right out. I waved, trying to get the guy's attention, so we could get off, but it was too late. The ride had already started. I took a deep breath to stay calm. As long as we were moving, it wasn't so bad. I counted the minutes until it was over. Then we reached the top and stopped. I'd forgotten about that. We sat at the top of the Ferris Wheel, our car swinging, and I held onto Ryan for dear life. It wasn't easy. He was a squirmy kid on a good day. What kind of mother was I? I risked the life of my toddler, because I couldn't tell him no. When we finally escaped the ride, I hugged Ryan tight, and almost kissed the ground in relief.

Flash forward twenty-two years. I was again at an amusement park. This time in Missouri, and there was a Ferris wheel. I stared up at it with trepidation. My grandson, Tyler, (Ryan's son) wanted to ride. He didn't understand why Nana wouldn't take him. I reasoned with myself, it would be fine. I wasn't pregnant this time, and the bar would go all the way down. I needed to get over my fear and this was my chance. I reluctantly agreed, and Tyler jabbered excitedly as we climbed into a car. We pulled the bar down, but it didn't stay there. It was locked but able to be moved a little up and down. How was this safe?

It was fine, I reasoned. I liked roller coasters. Sometimes. Once in a while. No one ever died from a Ferris Wheel, right? I should Google that. If I survived. We started moving, and at first it was fun. We swooped through the air, not really going that fast. Then came the part I always seemed to forget. The stop at the top that lasts way too long, while they unload passengers. Come on. Get those people off, already. Waiting for us to move again, I held onto Tyler, terrified. The car was swinging, and I started to panic. My heart beat faster, the air squeezing out of my lungs.

"Nana? What's wrong?"

His sweet eyes watched me, and I knew I had two options: Freak out and freak him out or pretend like I was enjoying the ride. There was only one real choice. I pointed out all the wonderful sights we could see high up in the air. When we finally got off, I hugged Tyler to me tightly and pledged never to do that again.

Which is why I couldn't really explain my current situation. I was a hundred and fifteen feet in the air over the historic Las Vegas strip, about to zipline. The tall tower we were on had no real walls, just metal everywhere. I was shaking, but it wasn't from fear. Not yet. I was cold. Anyone saying Vegas was nice, wasn't a hundred feet in the air at ten o'clock at night with an icy wind whipping around. I was apprehensive at first. We were told to be there promptly at nine or lose our spot. It gave us the false impression that this excursion would be quick. As a guy strapped the harness on me, I tried not to panic. What was I thinking? I was afraid of Ferris Wheels. Although I had explained that fact to my friend, Mandy, she was still able to talk me into it.

"You're not gonna stop," Mandy said, her adventurous spirit infectious. "You'll zip right through. It will only last a few minutes."

An hour and a half later, I'd lost much of my trepidation. I was too busy being cold and irritated, and wondering why it was taking so long. Once we got to the top row, we could see them strapping the harnesses to the zipline, and I realized the holdup. The zipliners went out four at a time. There was about fifty people on this row alone, and since it took ten to fifteen minutes for each group, we were going to be waiting another hour or so. Our friend, Shana, waited at the bottom for us, thinking it would only take about twenty minutes. We were going on several hours now. Shana was the practical one and wouldn't throw away fifty dollars for five minutes of fun. I couldn't blame her. In fact, I wished I was on the ground with her.

"Maybe we should just go." Mandy's arms were crossed, her teeth grinding together, whether from cold or anger I wasn't sure. Probably both. Still, she was the one who wanted to do this. "I didn't think it would take this long."

My heart leapt at her suggestion. Was I really going to chicken out now? "We've waited this long," I said. She agreed, and my chance to escape was gone.

Forty minutes later, we made it to the front. They separated us into four lines. Mandy was in the line next to me, and she gave me a thumbs up. I smiled, returning it, but my stomach was in knots. When they opened the chute for the groups ahead of us, I could see how far up we were and my pulse increased. I could do this. It had become my mantra over the last few hours. No one had died from this. Mandy had googled it. There was no reason for my fear.

They strapped the group in front of us onto the zipline, and I swallowed the lump in my throat. Once they were shot out of the chute, the ride operator motioned for me to move forward. I could do this, I repeated to myself, trying to believe it. After attaching me to the zipline, he added weights. I turned my head towards Mandy, and realized minutes from now, I would be hundreds of feet in the air. I'd had a panic attack once in my life. It felt like this. Air was escaping my lungs, but I couldn't draw it back in. My heart was thundering. My mantra abruptly changed.

"I can't do this," I said out loud to anyone who'd listen. "I can't do this." I shook my head, breathing becoming more difficult by the second. My voice held an edge of hysteria, and a full-on panic attack was only moments away.

The guy hooking me in, pulled on my strap. "Oh, you're doing this," he said. I realized they couldn't have people jumping ship at the last moment. Not with hundreds in line behind them. There was no way I was getting out of this. I tried to control my pounding heart. I didn't have a choice. I had to do this. Mandy gave me another thumbs up. I returned her gesture, my hand shaking. I was never listening to her again.

My stomach threatened to revolt. They'd had me bag up my glasses, so they wouldn't fall into the crowd. I wondered what they'd think about me losing my dinner over the tourists below. And then I couldn't think any more. The flap went up and I knew it was time. As an added twist of torture, they had us pushing off to propelling ourselves out into the night sky. I did as they asked. My only thought was getting this over with as quickly as possible. Suddenly, I was airborne. The dark blue sky was above, the crowd below, and it wasn't bad. Everything was blurry, but I could still see the people. I knew if I fell, I would die, but I felt secure. I was strapped in from my neck to my ankles. I put my hands out like I was flying, and a giddiness overcame me. I was doing this! I'd conquered my fear. I was ziplining. It was spectacular! The lights of Las Vegas were magical. I zipped over the crowd and then over a stage where an Eighty's hair band was singing, "Sweet Child of Mine." I was glad, in that moment, that I had done it. My happiness only lasted a minute, because as I neared the platform with the guys waiting to unhook us, my zipline slowed down. I was barely over the stage when I stopped completely. It didn't make sense. I could see the finish line, but I couldn't reach it. Mandy, and all the others, zipped past me, and I wondered why this was happening to me. I only stopped for a second. But I soon realized stopping wasn't that bad, because at that point, I started going backwards. As I gained momentum in the wrong direction, all I could do was stare at the people below. They were pointing at me and gesturing in the other direction as if to say, "No, go that way." Like I had a choice. I shrugged at them. What was I supposed to do? When

I was a quarter of the way back, I stopped again. This time I didn't move. I hung over the crowd, waiting for someone to rescue me, and it reminded me of the Ferris Wheel. At least, I didn't have a toddler with me. I thought that would make it easier. It didn't. I was there for hours, or minutes that felt like hours, my head hanging in defeat. Someone would come get me. All those people were at the top waiting for their turn. It seemed to take forever, and I said little prayer that if I made it out of there alive, I would be done with Ferris Wheels and ziplines and anything to do with heights, forever. After a while, most the people below me became bored with my predicament and moved on. A little boy waved at me. I waved back.

The line started jiggling and that was so much worse. I glanced up to see one of the zipline guys, upside down on the rope, crawling towards me. The Calvary had finally arrived.

"Ma'am?" he said. "How much do you weigh?"

I didn't expect that question, and I told him my usual weight. He didn't offer any platitudes. He just did his job and hooked on to me. He inched his way toward the end pulling me with him. Relief rushed through me as we reached the platform. Someone started unhooking my lines, and I couldn't wait to be out of the harness. My friend, Mandy, stood by watching and trying not to laugh.

"Ma'am? How much do you weigh?" the guy unhooking me asked. Why did everyone keep asking me that? What difference could it make now?

As I climbed down on wobbly legs, I again felt the urge to kiss the ground.

Mandy rushed up to me. "I'm so sorry," she said between laughs. "Of all the people to get stuck." She shook her head. "You'll never trust me again."

We reached the street, searching for Shana, and I thought about my experience. I'd never do it again, but I was still glad I'd done it. I'd conquered my fears. I ziplined through Vegas.

Mandy was already talking about her next adventure--jumping out of an airplane. "There's only one stop," she said. "The one at the bottom." What could go wrong?

Poetry

Poetry Judge

Missouri's first Poet Laureate and repeat poetry judge for *Well Versed*, Walter Bargen has published nineteen books of poetry. His most recent books are: *Days Like This Are Necessary: New & Selected Poems* (2009), *Endearing Ruins* (2012), *Trouble Behind Glass Doors* (2013), *Quixotic* (2014), *Gone West* (2014), and *Three-Corner Catch* (2015). His awards include a National Endowment of the Arts Fellowship (1991), *Quarter After Eight* Prose Prize (1996), the Hanks Prize (1996), the Chester H. Jones Foundation prize (1997), the William Rockhill Nelson Award (2005), Short Fiction Award–A cappella Zoo (2011). His poems, essays, and stories have appeared in over 300 magazines, including *American Literary Review, American Letters & Commentary, Beloit Poetry Journal, Denver Quarterly, Georgia Review, International Quarterly, Missouri Review, New Letters, New Novel Review, Pleiades, Poetry Northwest, River Styx, Seneca Review, Sycamore Review,* and *Witness.*

First Place **Poetry**

If I Could Whistle

Nancy Jo Allen

Ships, trains, bullets all whistle—
cars have *bells and whistles.*
A whistle begins and ends a factory
worker's day. If he is happy, he whistles
while he works. A referee begins and ends
a sports game with a whistle
as well as cries foul during a game.
Fire departments whistle to announce calls for help.
Whistling in the dark is a pessimistic act
with optimistic hope. Life guards
blow the whistle on bad behavior
in a pool, or warn of danger in the sea.
Men whistle at women and some women
take umbrage while some are validated—
it's in the ear of the beholder.

My tea kettle can whistle. Birds whistle
by instinct—not reason—to call lovers.
A dog whistle signals racism. Bing Crosby's
whistle was smooth as silk. Mother washed me
clean as a whistle. Once I blew the whistle
on a former employer—that was satisfying,
and the closest to whistling I may ever come.

Gabriel blows the whistle of a horn
gathering the dead. If I could whistle,
I would stick my fingers in my mouth
and blow like Dad did to call the dog,
but I would sit by the kitchen window
and wait for Dad to appear—not the dog.

Nancy Jo Allen is a Minnesota native who now lives in Columbia, Missouri. In recent years she enrolled in poetry courses at The Loft Literary Center of Minneapolis which has earned her publication in *Well Versed, * 82 Review, Dime Show Review,* and soon, *Third Wednesdays,* and *Firewords.* She has also been published in both Interpretations 4 and Interpretations 5, annual Columbia Art League projects of 2016 and 2017.

Second Place Poetry

If you had to go mad

Rebecca Graves

would you be like the Duchess of Devonshire and feed your chickens from a silver spoon? Feed them while gowned in taffeta and adorned by a choker of pearls?

Or, would you be like St. Francis, as artisans rendered him, downcast and hooded, cloaked in shadows, your pain seen as mercy?

If you had to go mad, would you slip off your clothes, slick down your hair, and don fake claws of brass?

Would you reach out like Adam, reaching through the centuries to a God you never quite touch?

If you had to go mad, would you turn your back to your home and walk down the highway, suitcase in hand?

Or, would you sit quietly in the kitchen, the clock ticking out time as you wait for pills to arrive in your mind. Would you fade from your friends, stay home, stay put, stay anything but sane? As if you had the choice.

And if you had to go mad, would you go like the Hatter, sharing tea with a hare, talking riddles to the air? Will time stop for you?

Or, would you put one foot forward, fake out your days in a mime of yourself.

If you had to go mad, would you?

Rebecca Graves has published several articles and book chapters in the world of academia where she works by day as a health sciences librarian. In her other life, she writes fiction and poetry which have been published in *Interpretations IV*, *Interpretations V*, as well as the anthology, *Eternal as a Weed: Tales of Ozark Experience* from Creative Writing of Columbia. Ms. Graves lives in Columbia, Missouri, with the inventor and jazz musician Pack Matthews.

The Storyseller

Kristian Wingo

In the shop, I held the story
The storyseller's pride and glory.
The good was as good as any I'd known,
Much much better than those of my own.

"This fable's falsified!" I cried.
"A legitimate legend this is not."

The storyseller balked,
scrubbed his bald spot,
adjusted his antique, creaky spectacles
and brushed his moustache's grey tentacles.

"It's fiction, you fool," he said, "Purely phony!"
"Genetically modified, made-up baloney.
But also genuine, homespun, hippocampus-baked,
one hundred percent human, and completely unfaked."

I tipped it, turned it, and made it bend.
I read it again from beginning to end.

"The details in here are much more fine-tuned
than the computer technology we take to the moon.
At Freytag's peak, how this damn thing twists!
Like a silicone screw turned by an onanist's wrists.
If this story's creator didn't rely on a robot
Or receive AI assistance for charting the plot,
Then I'm an avuncular orangutan."

He waited a moment, let my words hang,
Then laid into me with word-poisoned fang:
"Your shoddy stories may split at the seams,
And prick at one's fingers with their splintered scenes.
But *this* work sprouts purely from homo sapiens genes."

Assured he was wrong, I continued to goad:
"If Old Marco Polo had taken his load
Way past China, on the endless Silk Road,
Merged onto the Milky Way and then searched outer space,
He couldn't have found a thing of such grace.
These yarns are woven from fluff that's unknown
To our tiny galaxy's universe zone."

The smug seller's smile spanned his whole face,
"This gold can be found no matter the place,
You see, it was mined deep in the mind,
Go deep, deep, deep, and don't worry, you'll find."

I held it, beheld it, this curious story.
Microscopically grooved,
yet satin smooth.
Fine as sand,
yet pyramid grand.

"On second thought," I said to the vendor,
I'd like something without so much splendor.
I saw something else, round back, near that hovel.
Would you perchance sell me that dirty old shovel?"

Kristian Wingo is a teacher of English as a second language at the University of Missouri. He is originally from Champaign, Illinois.

Samuel Allin

Terry Allen

Born under the Blue Ridge
in the wild land
of game forests
and rushing waters
in a cabin
chinked with red mud,

he came into the world
of English and Irish descent,
subject to King George III
in that part of the realm
known as the Province
of North Carolina

and it was in the spring
or the summer of the year
that the big frost fell
in early May,
that he furnished
his own horse, rifle and gun
and went off to fight
for independency

and after the whole damn
hooptedoodle was over,
he lit out west with his family
to follow the deer
and wild game

and came to a little fertile valley,
encircled by hills
and decided to settle

and build a cabin
near a creek with plenty
of cedar, spruce and ash
along its banks, a good place
to spend the next thirty-eight years
tilling the soil, growing
thoroughbred horses
and prize cattle
and living on his own terms,
a self-dependent man,
subject to no king.

Many years later,
in a shady nook near a grove
of cedar and oak trees,
anyone who cared to
could find the graves
of Samuel and his wife Nancy,
their grandson Gilmer,
and three slaves.

North by Northwest

Gail Denham

North by Northwest

To climb down a President's
eyebrow on Mt. Rushmore
always gave Ruthie
the cold shivers.

When the Bistro played
that movie, she saved every
cent of her berry picking
money to see it four times.

Ruthie's Ma paid her a fine
compliment the day that film
left town. "You gotta' give
our Ruthie credit.

"She know how to dream,
that one. May amount to somethin'
one day, she keeps her heart tuned
and learns when it's time
to take chances."

A.C.

Larry Allen

The heating and air guys
Were at the house all that day
Grinding and drilling in the basement.

You would be amazed how
The inside units have gotten smaller
While the outside unit is huge.

Inside it looks like an oversized Zippo
Being engulfed by an octopus of pipes and ducts.

Outside you find some kind of cross
Between John Glenn's recovery module
And one of those teleportation pods from The Fly.

You expect any minute now
Jeff Goldblum will crack open the door
And call out, "Be afraid-be VERY afraid!"

But then perhaps
He is only talking about utility bills.

Little Baby Driver

Larry Allen

Little baby driver
Holds the yellow
Dashboard in her lap,
Pounds the horn,
Slams the accelerator
Tongue hanging out,
Imaginary tires scream.

Little driver
Grins broadly,
Sucks up her drool
And pounds the horn again,
More wheel turning
And button slamming
More squealing.

Little baby driver
Just fifteen years shy
Of her learner's permit.

Match.com

Larry Allen

Up all night emailing,
Inviting them to dinner,
Waving rare steaks in front of them.
Or breakfast,
Where the best country ham in town
Does battle with chipped cups and cracked glasses.

Still, I get no response

My daughter says maybe I come on too strong,
Like hey baby from the bushes strong
Panting and drooling on the World Wide Web.
So I tone it down.
More Roger Moore, less Lon Chaney.

But still I get no response.

Why can't they say SOMETHING,
Like, I' m already in a relationship'"
Or "I just don't feel the vibe".
Or "I have a horrible hang nail today".

But nothing.

They remind me of the Sphinx,
Brooding and silent,
But somehow still
As mysterious as all heck.

A Nocturne

Nancy Jo Allen

Ice tumbles into the freezer tray
in the kitchen. The house
moans as the northwest corner

settles onto the foundation
and the shower head
drips just one *plop.*

Conditioned air hums,
sinking softly atop quilts
that cover our bodies

entwined where we
warm one another. You
sleep—deaf ear up.

A truck rumbles past
on the highway to the north,
while wind chimes

tinkle their tympani
in sweet night air
thick and dark as molasses.

You add to this larghetto
as you breathe
purring steady notes—

I am here.

I am here.

We are here.

Paring it Down

Nancy Jo Allen

The peel hangs from the tip of the knife—
one long curly-cue of red and green—
over the gaping maw of the disposal
about to be fed. The paring drops into the abyss
which eats greedily with one flick of the wall switch.
The knife now cuts through the apple
pulp making four large, fresh chunks
he sets in a red bowl after removing the stem,
core and pips.

It's routine before settling into the recliner—
brown and stuffed near the fireplace—
to watch TV at the end of a long day
of healthy choices intended to clean excess sugars
from his blood. He plans to stay with me
many more years and I watch his fist
rise to his mouth as he looks at me—
his fingers push the fruit
between his smiling lips.

drifting away

Terry Allen

they stand at the top of the hill
in each other's arms

under the quarter moon
dimmed by falling snow

silhouetted by one
haloed streetlamp

winter has been busy
the street is banked and white

a gust of wind picks up
and fresh flakes swirl about them

years pass
the couple marries

memories fade
he visits her now

in a home that's not theirs
where her mind sometimes drifts

to a winter night
when the Lady of Time

brought the purest
white flying carpet

that took them for a ride
into their adult lives

Typhoon

Terry Allen

No ballast.
An empty ship.
At night.

Pounded by powerful winds
and towering walls of water
rolls thirty degrees heeled on one side.

Then whips to thirty degrees heeled
on the other side in mere seconds.

The teeth of the storm
spits rain and flashes lighting
as thunder rolls across the dark sea.

The ship's hull slams into the troughs
between the waves
as the captain and crew turn
the great vessel,
pointing its bow into the tempest
plowing forward
and on toward the lights of home.

Before and After

Karen Mocker Dabson

Before

Babes and balmy breezes blow
Across the beach, along the shore
Where we have tarried hours more
Than is our usual

But school starts up again next week
And soon enough their little feet
Bound in new shoes, both tight and neat
Will bid the sand farewell

The radio calls out, "Escape!"
But we have seen all this before,
So grabbed some beer and milk and more
Ere coming to the beach

Now lightning spangles twixt the clouds
And dragon wind in fury blasts
We chase kids and chairs within its grasp
And tender our retreat

Stuffed snugly in our old sedan
The lashing rain does not delay
Our arrival home, where we will stay
To watch the storm go by

The TV pumps out kid cartoons
The children, dry, sit on the couch
Grape popsicles slurped in their mouths
Pup sleeping by their side.

After

Dry once more on the convention center floor
The kids slurp thumbs in dreaming
Wrapped in itchy, warm gray blankets
Curled like kittens on their cotton cots.

God knows what images burn behind those eyes
Was it the element of surprise when
Foreign waters opened the front door
Pushing into every corner of our lives

Randomly destroying toys, TV
Soaking their precious drawings carefully
Placed and held by alphabet magnets
On the refrigerator door?

Or was it that last view of puppy's black head
As she swept through the window
Frantically pawing for purchase
As a churning wave bore her to sea?

Or could it be, sitting in the dinghy that we
Had finally allowed to save us,
The sight of our rooftop, like some great inverted
Galley, gliding away through the muddy waters?

Rest, my sweet children
And find what peace you may
Daddy and I will work on the worry
Wondering where tomorrow will be.

Detail: Roadside Table

Karen Mocker Dabson

White Wonder Bread
  Perennially present at our picnics
  Perennially on sale
Its sliced, square sides
  Mayonnaise-glued to
Big, round slabs of Jumbo
  Bologna and pickle constructions

The bread dimples
  Beneath my fingertips
While red flecks festoon
  Billy's lips, blood-like
Ketchup spatters
  Squeezed from the wounds
  Of martyred sandwiches.

Looking On

Gail Denham

The place rocked. Rotating ball lights
colored dancers green, red, golden
yellow. My ears vibrated deep
to the bone. The energy on that
dance floor, harnessed,
could power a small town.

Had I ever been this young,
this carefree, this wild? Through
the haze I saw a lone figure
sipping a soda, watching.
Was he a father come to shepherd
his daughter safely home, or even
through the parking lot to her car,

where now even low-riders sans mufflers
and Harleys gunning power under their hoods
seemed almost peaceful. Slowly I backed away;
looked back, remembered my one-speed pedal
bicycle rides on quiet country roads, where birds
were in no danger of my cruising speed.

Treasured Imagination

Gail Denham

Don't splash water on parents. Perhaps
I'm a pirate ship billowing in on the tide,
loaded with loot. Watch out! My hull
sends massive waves to the beach.

Imagination is a precious gift. It happens
to us all. I secure mine deep inside, coddle
it, nurse it, give it air at times, let it speak
to my soul.

Imagination bursts, colors our world
in beauteous hues, traps stories of adventure
on pages, takes us to watch pageants
of characters, expressing
profundities and fun.

Whenever possible, I roam. With me, imagination
breathes fresh air from mountains, wood smoke
on autumn afternoons. Sometimes I watch it sop
up a swirling story. I take it for walks in the woods,
hold its hand, ask what I missed, if anything.

My desire is to write with imagination that flows
from every pore; share as if it were Christmas
morning. Offer it gift-wrapped in warm words
which might bring others with me on the journey.

Perhaps I'll even splash a little
at my family, snip off portions
and send them around the world
to help folks imagine.

Silent Witness

Rebecca Graves

After dark, stand under the streetlight
alone.
Watch the snow fall.
Each crystal its own,
together a blue blanket over winter grass.
The silence a twin to the night.
Night swept clean in the circle of light.

Inside, shades close darkness in.
The floor lamp warms the room,
a cosseted space, a den of darkness to burrow in.

Daylight leaves a life wide open,
a broad expanse of tasks and chores,
of snow covered fields.
Full sun throws shadows and questions,
all sharp edges and well defined,
casts us outside, no excuses.

The shifts change at dusk: creatures
going to ground, taking to sky.
Souls are loose then, untethered, an unsettling in-between.
The sinking of the sun strikes sorrow in the gut,
a restless rise of pulse, a hint of the end.

Wrap darkness in light.
Keep a flame burning until evening folds in.
Feel the scurrying settle as nights tents out.
Wrapped in the swaddling of lamp light breath out:
after the dark, the end comes, and you're still here.

You Wore Blue, The Germans Wore Grey

Rodnie McHugh

I can't remember if it were cotton or silk,
   that blouse you wore the last time we kissed.

What I do remember is the feel of your skin,
   so s m o o t h and warm beneath the cloth.

  O, to touch
    your alabaster softness without
       fabrical hindrance;

  O, to caress
    your silken glow
      unimpeded by material obstruction.

I can't remember if it were muslin or chinz,
   but blue was its color an' genteel the pattern
        -----that chemise you wore.

But what does it matter if I can't remember the cloth?
    I do remember the last time we kissed.

  In hushed silence Rommel returned from Afrika.

Rewired, Inspired

Heidi Mouat Mendez

Quiet will
Being still

A fresh start
Silent heart

Peaceful day
Time replay

Taking break
Plans to make

Serene rest
Before quest

Treasure hear
Open ear

Soar

Heidi Mouat Mendez

To exotic places you can fly away,
Like Guatemala, Jamaica, and the Bay,
And, young spirit, that's okay.

Wandering, always searching for something more,
But remember, my child, when your wings get sore,
Fly your soul back to my door.

"I would prefer that you come back."

Runaway

Heidi Mouat Mendez

Music falling, incomplete,
Sitting on unstable seat.

Responsibilities weigh,
Systematic runaway.

Seeing with a different eye,
Visions, dreams, welcoming why.

All at once, too many things,
Watching birds with saving wings.

Like rebels running wild,
But boldly, treasures smiled.

Bending but not broken yet,
Holding fast for one not met.

All together they would stay,
Not finished, but on their way.

Mama's Soundtrack

Billie Mulkey

Sounds of Life
Unfolding down the years
Stored away in memory
Sharp, crisp and clear

Once more they play
Mama yells
Don't slam that
Screen door!

Baby wailing
Children's laughter
Scuffling feet
Cops and robbers
Bang! Bang!
Shoot 'em up

Phone is ringing
Doggie barking chasing cars
Radios blaring
Engines revving, sirens screaming
Above it all
Mama singing

Noonday whistle slices air
Footsteps running
Freight train warning
Mama yelling
Whipping egg whites
Don't slam that screen door!

Choo-choo trains
Whistles, horns
Baby dolls crying
Little toy drums

Christmas morning symphony

Guitars strumming on the porch
Happy yodeling
Marching bands
Folks all cheering
Voices raised for evening harmony

Slap slap wipers clearing glass
Fats Domino singing
Blueberry Hill
Bluejay scolding
World unfolding
All of it
Ineffable thrill

Screen door slams
For the last time
No one took notice
How silent it seems
On Mama's soundtrack
Of unfinished dreams

The Things a Mother Tucks Away

Billie Mulkey

All the little things
A Mother tucks away
Are especially saved
For that far-off Someday

Someday
All the photos will strut
In paired off kind
Across the pages
Of an album
Like they are
In Mother's mind

Someday
All the little
Books and drawings
Made by chubby hands
Will have a special place
Such works of Art demand

Someday
All the delicate trinkets
And dime store bric-a-brac
Will have a
Regal home
Displayed upon
Moms see-all-rack

Someday
All graduation cards
Christmas cards
And birthday greetings
Will fill a scrapbook
Chock full
Of moments oh so fleeting

Someday the things
A mother tucks away
Would fill all
The ships at sea
Someday must
Of necessity be
Always moving on

Someday became yesterday
Overnight
The little things
A mother tucked away
Comfort now and speak
Of love
Treasured and gathered
In a yielding past

Mondays in October

Sheree K. Nielsen

Worried minds
and tense bodies
melt away
with the simple brush
of an ocean breeze
across eburnean cheeks.

Little girls named Remy
donning jacinthe and white-striped
bathing suits
with messy blonde hair,
sandy toes,
and sticky fingers
sipping strawberry-kiwi
pouch drinks
plop down
on opaque aqua
spaghetti-webbed
chaise lounges
become your best friend
at the beach,
on Mondays
in October.

Visual Perceptions

Sheree K. Nielsen

The sunless sky
appears a misty haze
blurring
structures,
figures,
and natural
phenomenon,
beside the shore.

Sand
mimics the sea
as ripples
of white,
pewter
and celery green
intermingle
with shadows cast
by midday sun.

Clouds form
cotton candy pillows
tittering the atmosphere.
Seagulls
wistfully,
blissfully
soar above
the horizon.

My mind wanders
to easy days
and lazy nights
where campfires
linger
and glow,
conversations
flow
and time
takes
a much
needed
nap.

Raspberry Point

Sheree K. Nielsen

At dusk,
I amble
a footpath
of mulch
and moist soil,
pungent
with humidity,
and the buzzing
cacophony
of
annoying
mosquitoes.

Lush,
citrine
Cinnamon and royal ferns,
low lying grasses,
and mosquitoes
brush
tender ankles
as I perambulate
the eerie
spruce bog.

Dark evergreens,
wild crimson raspberries
and fungi
abound
in this inexplicable
mystery.

I wait
for the
Creature
From the Black Lagoon,
but he
never
comes . . .

The Somnambulist

Marsha Posz

A poem based on Cora Mowatt, famous for her strong personality and ability to predict what treatments would work for her physical illnesses when she was mesmerized by her physician during the age of Victorian Spirituality.

Hemorrhages attack my lungs,
but no man may assign a diagnosis
of hysterics to my condition.
I refuse to be assigned to the settee,
ankles crossed in propriety,
voluminous skirts arranged in perfection.

You mesmerize me?
Ah, but I have mastered my own medicine.
I assign the cure and will not merely be
your somnambulist as you lecture those around you.
You seem to feel threatened, and perhaps
it is my assertions and knowledge which do so.

I shall awaken as I choose, days, or weeks from now.
When I do, I shall, unfortunately, return to the meek,
the mild, the feminine.
But until then, I am your equal
with intellect, strength, and vivacity.
Perhaps the hysterics reside in you. My other self is nothing
and the time for me is just beginning.

A Legacy

Eva Ridenour

Spider webs of Queen Anne's lace
dance along the highway.

A few feet away, chicory waves in the cool
morning breeze, each blossom as blue as a baby's eyes.

A clump of bright yellow Lazy Susan smiles up
at passersby through dark centers, lighting the day.

What once were weeds hidden in trash and rubble along the road
have become beautiful breaks in weeds and grasses

just like first lady, Lady Bird Johnson dreamed.

Poison Ivy

Eva Ridenour

"It just needs a little tender loving care,"
the prospective buyer said as we
walked through the house.
He'd fix it up and rent it—
his twenty-seventh property.

First thing he did was doze the fence,
bushes and everything close to the house.

I'm sure he planned to rent it by summer,
but he got sick. Took more than a month
to tear that old shed down where I stored my
lawnmower, and they gutted the house.

I lived there for fourteen and a half years.
It's where I first learned I was allergic to poison ivy.
I loved the forsythia in late March.
Came to finally remember the casc ades of pink
blossoms in April were on a wisteria.
Enjoyed the old-time spirea in early May
and a few weeks later the mock-orange bloomed,
smelled, just like damp desert after a spring rain.

In spite of everything, a few of the irises
I hadn't moved bloomed.

The other day I passed by.
The poison ivy I fought
is nearly up to the window on the north side.
I guess that's what
"tender loving care" means.

Grandma's Wish

Eva Ridenour

Mom always called her a saint
for what she put up with from her menfolk.
An orphan, taken in by her maternal
grandfather when her parents died,
didn't have much say-so about her life.

Her grandfather married her off just
soon as she got old enough.
My grandfather came into his
lumberyard, where she worked
and asked for her hand.
Her grandpa gave no thought to
the fact she could have taught school.
She was another mouth to feed.

Ten children later, after a less than happy
fifty-year marriage, she stood outside their
rented house where my grandfather had just
died and wondered how she would live
without someone telling her what to do.

Her two bachelor sons took care of this
when raising hogs gave way to cholera.
They, with her, moved to our town
more than one-hundred miles away.

During the winter, in the living room
of the three-roomed house next door to us,
the sons cleaned game, muskrats, mink,
raccoons, an occasional opossum, rabbit
or squirrel in front of the stove.
They stretched the skins, that eventually dried,
and left them where they'd cure quickly so
they could sell them.

Grandma slept near the stench every night.
All she'd ever hoped for was a house
where someone didn't have
to sleep in the living room.

Effingham

Barry Walker

It was the painted dream.
The sunshine, the starlight, and silvery moon spilled like acrylic paint.
Washes and hues stained my lips.
It was better than my first high school kiss.
Outside, the billboards advertised Cat Crap kingdom, and Bob Evans doggy
sausages.
Making it the best damn breakfast in mid-Missourah!
The mistletoe shined in my eyes.
I had a live butterfly in my house.
Outside, opaque mist and ice drenched the ground.
Cars turned into a graveyard of vehicles.
The corpse flower bloomed, and the crashed cars gathered to pollinate it
But I had my own sweet nectar.
Secret, private, away from prying eyes, it was you.

goodbye, my friend

Adria Waters

mischievous yellow eyes
staring out from under the rocking chair
greeting me in the morning
purring warm bundle in my lap
cloudy yellow eyes
peering out through the metal bars
closing for the last time
loving lick as she fades away
goodbye, my friend

Author Bios

Larry W. Allen has had poems published in *Main Street Rag, The Hatchet, Fine Arts Discovery, Mid-America Poetry Review, Interpretations 4*, and other publications. His book, *Do Come In And Other Lizzie Borden Poems* was published by Pear Tree Press. The poem, *Mr. Snapper Flapper*, won Judges Choice for poetry in *Well Versed 2016*.

After over twenty years in area broadcasting, Larry retired as a Missouri Probation and Parole Officer.

Nancy Jo Allen is a Minnesota native who now lives in Columbia, Missouri.

In recent years she has taken poetry courses at The Loft Literary Center of Minneapolis which has earned her publication in *Well Versed, * 82 Review, Dime Show Review*, and soon, *Third Wednesdays*, and *Firewords*. She has also been published in both *Interpretations 4* and *Interpretations 5*, annual Columbia Art League projects of 2016 and 2017.

Terry Allen is an Emeritus Professor of Theatre Arts at the University of Wisconsin-Eau Claire, where he taught acting, directing and playwriting. He directed well over a hundred plays during his thirty-eight years of teaching. A few favorites include: *Candide, Macbeth, Death of a Salesman*, and *The Threepenny Opera*. He now plays pickleball and writes poetry and has been published in *I-70 Review, Freshwater Poetry Journal, Skylark Review, Chariton Review, Third Wednesday, Star 82 Review, The Avalon Literary Review, Common Ground Review, Modern Poetry Quarterly Review, Main Street Rag* and others.

Drew Coons met his wife Kit while living in Africa to do non-profit humanitarian work in 1980. "Kit was living in a mud house with a metal roof and no running water or electricity," Drew recalls. "She is as tough as a hickory nut." There Kit taught in a teachers college while Drew worked as an engineer to provide clean water to nineteen cities and towns.

As humorous speakers specializing in strengthening relationships, the Coonses have taught in every part of the US and in thirty-seven other countries. For two years, they lived and taught in New Zealand and Australia. They are keen cultural observers and incorporate their many adventures into their writing and speaking.

Karen Mocker Dabson has written a debut novel called *The Muralist's Ghost* for which she received the Missouri Writers Guild's 2015 Walter Williams award, second place, recognizing "research or high literary quality involved in the creation of a major work."

Some of her short stories and poems have appeared in the anthologies of the Columbia Chapter of the Missouri Writers Guild and several editions of the *Story Circle Journal*. She has received writing awards from both organizations. She has published in the Mozark Press's 2014 *That Mysterious Woman* and the Columbia Art League's *Interpretations* anthologies several times, and won first place for poetry in 2017 from the Missouri Writers Guild.

Originally from Pittsburgh, Pennsylvania, Dabson, formerly of Columbia, Missouri, now lives with her husband, Brian, in Durham, North Carolina, and is currently completing her second and third novels.

Cortney Daniels received her undergraduate and Masters' degrees from University of Missouri and is a graduate of the Iowa Writers' Workshop with an MFA in Poetry. Currently, she is working on a book of creative nonfiction.

She has three grown children and a grandchild who all live elsewhere. She lives in Columbia, Missouri, with her spouse and cats, and works at a local nonprofit organization.

Gail Denham's poetry, stories, news articles and photos were published in magazines, books, anthologies for close to forty years. Poetry and short stories are now her main focus. Denham's a member of many poetry societies and leads writing workshops.

"Poets look for inspiration in the smallest object," says Denham. Married, with four sons and many grandchildren, Denham uses adventure trips for inspiration.

Ida Bettis Fogle lives in Columbia, Missouri. She has been writing stories, poems and essays since childhood, and currently has a novel in progress. Her work has appeared in a variety of publications, including the literary magazines, *Well Versed* and *Mid-America Poetry Review*, and anthologies, *Eternal as a Weed: Tales of Ozark Experience*, *Uncertain Promise*, *Coming Home*, and *Boundless*. Her poem, *First Time Out*, was runner-up in the 2017 LED Contest, sponsored by Partial Press and the *Columbia Daily Tribune*.

Rebecca Graves has published several articles and book chapters in the world of academia where she works by day as a health sciences librarian. In her other life, she writes fiction and poetry which have been published in *Interpretations IV*, *Interpretations V*, as well as the anthology, *Eternal as a Weed: Tales of Ozark Experience from Creative Writing of Columbia.*

Ms. Graves lives in Columbia, Missouri, with the inventor and jazz musician Pack Matthews.

At seventeen, **Millicent Porter Henry** vowed to escape rural Iowa for exotic places. And so she did. Yet the Midwest pulls her back again and again to its great plains where the words flow wild and free like the rivers, and stories beg to be shared. Today she lives and writes in Columbia, Missouri with her husband of too many years—well within striking distance of grandchildren. Her work appears in a variety of publications.

Susan Koenig writes short stories and novels. Her fiction has appeared in *Well Versed* and the Columbia Art League's *Interpretations IV*, a pairing of artists and writers. She enjoys time spent with family and friends and lives in Columbia, Missouri with her husband.

Rodnie McHugh was born in Los Angeles, California where he pursued his undergraduate education. After earning his B.A. he spent a decade in the work force before moving to Columbia in 1981, where he earned his M.A. in History from the University of Missouri-Columbia He stayed on at UMC for five years working in administration at Jesse Hall. By 1990, he found his niche teaching world history at Hickman High School. Since his retirement in 2014 he has written his first novel, and has been published in *Well Versed*.

Lynn McIntosh is well into her sixties, lost some of her mind and none of her weight raising five sons in Columbia Missouri. She remains in Columbia writing about somethings and nothings that come to her mind, before it is all gone. She would like to tell her friends and extended family what she thinks, but they have regrettably stopped asking. So she writes it down.

Heidi Mouat Mendez received her Bachelor of Arts degree in Studio Arts from Lawrence University in Appleton, Wisconsin, in 1990. She is an avid personal journal writer and has enjoyed taking several correspondence and online writing courses through the Institute of Children's Literature, Writers' Digest, and Creative Non-Fiction while raising her children. She enjoys illustrating her poems in pencil and colored pencil. The poems submitted here are from what she calls the "Come Back" series. She currently resides in Jefferson City and spends much of her time in Columbia, drinking coffee and writing.

Frank Montagnino is a retired ad man blown out of New Orleans and into the clutches of the CCMWG by Hurricane Katrina. If you're reading this, it means his partly true story made it into the anthology. He hopes you enjoy it.

Chinwe I. Ndubuka's flash fiction works have been published in *Well Versed*, as well as *Interpretations I* and *Interpretations II*, anthologies of paired literary and visual works selected by the Columbia Art League. Another won a themed flash fiction contest organized by the Daniel Boone Regional Library. Chinwe I. Ndubuka writes from Missouri where she also works in environmental science.

At age ninety-three, **Billie Mulkey** enjoys listening to audiobooks and telling her family stories from the Depression era, WWII and the fabulous fifties. She still finds small notepads and loose sheets of poetry that she tucked away in boxes and drawers from each decade of her life. It is a joy to share them now. Billie loves people, conversation and good strong coffee!

Sheree K. Nielsen, Author/Photographer/Poet, is the recipient of the 2015 Da Vinci Eye Award for *Folly Beach Dances*, a 'healing' coffee table book inspired by the sea and her lymphoma journey. Publications include South and North Brunswick Magazine, Missouri Life, Southern Writers Magazine, among others. *Midnight, The One-Eyed Cat*, a picture book about overcoming handicaps, is slated for fall 2018 (Amphorae). When not writing, she's discovering new coffeehouses and beaches with her goofy canine kids and husband. www.shereenielsen.wordpress.com

Suzanne Connelly Pautler started dabbling with writing during her childhood years while growing up in both St. Louis County, then rural Franklin County, Missouri. She is an avid reader, genealogy detective, historical presenter, and nature lover. As a life-long learner, she has a passion for researching a variety of topics, particularly those related to history and travel. She and her husband reside in Columbia, Missouri.

Von Pittman retired after a career in Distance and Continuing Education at four state flagship and land grant universities. He began writing fiction just prior to retirement. His stories have appeared in numerous regional anthologies and national magazines, including *The First Line, Perspectives Magazine, Iowa History Illustrated, Cantos,* and *The Cuivre River Review.*

Eva Ridenour started her writing career by writing magazine articles. She has written and published nine romance novels under the pen name of Elizabeth Butler. *Libby* is the 2004 Walter Williams Missouri Writers Guild Award winner. Her poetry has appeared in *Cappers, The Mid-America Poetry Review* and *Well Versed.* She is past-president and secretary of CCMWG and past-treasurer of the Missouri Writers Guild. A retired secretary from Illinois, she lives in Fayette, Missouri.

Kit Salter lived many places in his early life—twenty-two addresses between birth and high school graduation. He went to a small college in northern Ohio, and attended graduate school at the University of California, Berkeley. He taught geography for twenty years at UCLA, and fourteen years at Mizzou (chair all the while) and consulted for the National Geographic Society for ten years. However, the best move he ever made in seventy-nine years was meeting, courting, and marrying Cathy Riggs forty years ago. He has written fiction off and on for decades.

Stephen Paul Sayers is a writer of horror and supernatural thriller fiction. He holds a Ph.D. from the University of Massachusetts and is a professor at the University of Missouri. Stephen has completed one novel, and his fiction has appeared in *Unfading Daydream.* He divides his time between Columbia, Missouri and Cape Cod, Massachusetts writing and teaching.

Billie Holladay Skelley worked as a Clinical Nurse Specialist providing postoperative care for cardiothoracic surgery patients. As a nursing educator, she has written several health-related articles for both professional and lay journals. Now retired from nursing, Billie enjoys focusing on her writing. Her poems, articles, and essays have appeared in various journals, magazines, and anthologies in print and online. An award-winning author, she also has written books for children and teens.

Jana Stephens has been retired since 2003; she formerly worked as an RN. She and her husband live just outside Columbia. Some of her stories are based on her mother's life. Jana also writes extensively of observations and experiences while traveling alone throughout Mexico City and outlying cities. She is grateful to her writers' group for their support, encouragement, and recommendations. She would have put an adverb before 'grateful' but couldn't think of one that was superlative enough.

Deb Sutton enjoys writing annoying characters who never do as they're told, much like her children. Her first novel, Broken Sidewalks, was published in 2015. She's previously been published in the 2015, 2016, and 2017 editions of *Well Versed.* Her second novel, Trial & Error will be available in 2018. She enjoys dabbling in many genres, including Non-Fiction and Poetry.

Barry Walker writes poetry, science-fiction, and fantasy. He is entering his novel *The Gar-Face* to the SEMO Writers Contest this November.

Adria Waters is the author of the Ghost Hunters Society series and has seen ghosts all her life. She loves exploring the paranormal and goes on ghost tours in every place she visits. When she's not hunting ghosts, she loves torturing her family with road trips across the country to see every single sightseeing opportunity in the United States. Adria lives in Missouri with her very patient husband, her not so patient son, two cats who insist that they are human, and various little spirits that pop up to say "hello" once in a while.

Cam Wheeler writes short stories, essays and poetry. Her work has appeared in *Well Versed, Inside Columbia* magazine and on therumpus.net. She is an eager traveler with eclectic tastes in literature, music and cinema. She resides in Mid-Missouri where an affable doodle allows her to share his home.

Kristian Wingo is a teacher of English as a second language at the University of Missouri. He is originally from Champaign, Illinois.

These days **Lori Younker** explores the worlds of fiction and memoir. Two short story collections, *Mongolian Interior* and *Sioux Beside Me,* seek to capture her cross-cultural experiences. Many stories can be accessed at WorldSoBright.org.

Lori used her Master's degree in TESOL at the Graduate School of Missouri University (2010-2014) and currently as an instructor of ELLs in the public schools of Mexico, Missouri where she teaches children her first love: to read and write.

The Columbia Chapter
of the Missouri Writers' Guild

The Columbia Chapter of the Missouri Writers' Guild has served the writers of Central Missouri since 1959. We sponsor a variety of activities throughout the year to provide writers both the encouragement to keep writing and the opportunity to perfect their craft.

We invite anyone who writes or wants to write to join in our efforts by becoming a member of the CCMWG. Our membership is diverse, representing many literary genres and levels of both ambition and accomplishment. Writers who want merely to write for their own enjoyment and self-expression are as welcome as those who regularly find publishers for their work.

Read about our current activities, including monthly meetings and our series of Show Me Writers Masterclasses at **ccmwg.org**.